M000316255

Princess

Sapphire Knight

PRINCESS

Cover Design by CT Cover Creations
Editing by Mitzi Carroll
Formatting by Max Effect

Dedicated to:

My serial readers.
Thank you for sticking with me!

If you've read all my previous books,
I hope this one knocks your socks off.

ALSO BY
Sapphire

OATH KEEPERS MC SERIES

Secrets
Exposed
Relinquish
Forsaken Control
Friction
Princess
Sweet Surrender

RUSSKAYA MAFIYA SERIES

Secrets
Corrupted
Unwanted Sacrifices
Russian Roulette

STANDALONES

Unexpected Forfeit
1st Time Love
(Coming Soon)

Warning

This novel includes graphic language and adult situations. It may be offensive to some readers and includes situations that may be hotspots for certain individuals. This book is intended for adults 18 and older.

This work is fictional. The story is meant to entertain the reader and may not always be completely accurate.

FREQUENTLY USED
Terms

NOMAD

MC member with no permanent home/wanderer

CHURCH

MC sit down to discuss business

COMPOUND

MC clubhouse/living area/office

OL' LADY

Significant other to MC member

CLAIM/LAYING CLAIM

Becoming responsible for another in the eyes of the club/ Announcing your property/taking your woman

One

VIKING

SAVAGE. THAT'S WHAT MY MOTHER CALLED ME GROWING up—a no good, filthy savage. I didn't know it at the time, but she was right.

If finding an ounce of pleasure by causing others pain makes me one, then so be it. I'll own that title because it's true. I fucking love pulling the skin away from others' flesh as they scream in agony.

I wish I could say that I haven't always been this way, but that would be a lie. Not that I'm above lying; if anything, I'll use it freely whenever it benefits me. For example, when I found this MC, I didn't come by it with any good intentions.

Arriving tired and irritated, I was sent by an MC called The Widow Makers. They wanted me to take out some rival Oath Keeper member whose road name was Exterminator. I was told that he had murdered some important members from another club—The Southern Outlaws.

The few SO Members that were left alive warned me multiple times during our meeting about how Exterminator's a ruthless killer, and I should watch him before making my move. Of course, I was planning on some recon; anyone who's been paid to kill before knows that shit. If anything, I was overconfident. Had it been me sent on the run to eliminate the Southern Outlaws, none of them would have been left alive.

After scouting Exterminator for a few days, I showed up at the bar he'd visited every night. I figured if I got there early, I'd have the one up on him.

My plan started to go to shit when I got into it with another club. The members had gotten me down on the ground, and I was struggling. I can handle three okay, but more than three I have to work at it.

Three of them had been taking turns at kicking out my right knee and then, in the end, striking me in the back with a metal stool to get me to fall. Once I hit the floor, five guys were on me like fucking leeches. They were determined to teach me a lesson but too big of pussies to do it one-on-one.

Exterminator and his boys stumbled into the middle of it all and bailed my ass out. Why? I'll most likely never know. They aren't the friendly type to most, but for some reason chose to have my back.

He saved my life that night. I didn't even know it was him until after it was too fucking late. Once a man saves your life, you don't take his cash—no matter what amount is offered.

The brothers helped me out, putting me up for as long as I needed. They were clueless, not knowing that I had my own means to make it. In time, they opened up some and showed me a brotherhood that I didn't know existed.

They aren't like the other clubs I'd been around. The Nomads from the Oath Keepers MC were all about themselves, but also each other. They never acted individually, but whole like a team.

With time, I was offered a spot to ride with them. It was hands down the best decision I've ever made.

I've never admitted my true reasons for going to the bar that night and my brothers have never pried. Eventually, though, I know my dirty deeds will catch up to me; they're always in the wind, riding my tail, waiting for me to fuck up and come barreling out.

The Nomads run differently than the rest of the clubs; we're freer. We don't belong to one Charter but float around to wherever we're needed or feel like going. The regular clubs' rules don't necessarily apply to our group. We have a structure amongst us, but not as strict as the Charters. A few of the brothers like Texas a lot, so we end up spending most of our time here when we stop for a bit. Otherwise, we keep on the move, rarely staying at one place for too long.

Scot and Exterminator pretty much call the shots when it comes down to things; otherwise, we work more as a unit. Ironic since we don't play well with others often. None of us own much; it makes it easier to travel.

We aren't tied down by any women either. Scot had an Ol' Lady at one point, but when she passed on, he went Nomad. That was before I was around, though. Exterminator and Nightmare don't talk much about if they had an Ol' Lady in the past or not.

I'm fairly young compared to them, so I'm all about playing the field when presented with getting my cock sucked. Pussy's another thing entirely; it's gotta be worth it for me to get in it.

Ex and Night are pretty tight with each other; they handle a lot of shit together. It's not quite as excessive as Saint and Sinner; sometimes I wonder if they wipe each other's asses with how close those two are. They seem to share everything—room, food, women; they don't have any boundaries when it comes to the other.

Spider's pretty quiet most of the time, and Ruger just likes to shoot the shit. All in all, we make up our small group and we're each just fucked up enough to compliment the other.

Occasionally, we'll get a full-time member who transfers over to us, but they never last. Men all bitch that they want freedom, but then many can't handle the level of freedom that we have. We don't follow your everyday lifestyle; we say fuck the bullshit and do what we want.

We have our unspoken set of rules amongst the group that we follow. The main ones being: We don't rape women, we don't kill anyone innocent, we always have each other's backs, we never interrupt a fight unless someone feels we might die, and well, that's pretty much it.

Nancy, the bartender, sets a tall draft in front of me as my ass hits the seat. Immediately taking a large swig, I down half of the refreshing beverage, parched from the Texas heat. Saving the rest for the next drink, my glass hits the top with a thud.

My brothers quickly follow and place their empty cups back on the counter. Feeling a little more relaxed as we all settle into our favorite shitty roadside bar. We always stop in when we're visiting central Texas.

We just got back here; we were off on a run to California. The brothers and I were helping out the local Chapter here. They were having an issue with a notorious club known as the Iron Fists.

It all turned out to be a success, as we sat by and watched those fuckers burn to death. I enjoyed every minute of torching that ratty clubhouse with them locked inside. That's what they get for fucking with the wrong crew. The Oath Keepers are well known for their loyalties when it comes to family, so this other club should have taken note. That's their fuck up, though, and in the end, they paid the ultimate price with their lives.

No sweat off my back, though. I couldn't give a fuck when it comes to killing scum. People around me thought I was a heartless bastard, and they're probably right about that. I don't have the guilty conscience eating me up inside like others get; I've seen too much and done too many things.

Taking a life is simple—almost poetic watching the life drain from their eyes. Why should I feel bad for removing them from a fucked up world anyhow? No one ever saved me, so in a way, I'm doing them a favor.

"Ye good, laddie?" Scot gestures to my neck, and I nod with an irritated grunt.

Ares, the VP of the local Chapter, and I got into it the other day. The fight wasn't anything serious, but he put his hands around my throat and left a mark. He was making Ex look bad in Church, and I wasn't having it; no one needs to make my brothers or myself look incapable. If anything, we're more than capable when it comes to handling things, and we should get more credit when it's due.

"Yep, I'm straight. Don't get it why they didn't just let us settle it, though. Now shit's unfinished, and I wanna have a turn to prove my point."

"I'm guessin' they put a stop to it, as it was their Church time. As for Ares, ye should just stick to yer own. No good will come from messing with the VP."

"Oh, I can handle my own, trust."

"Aye, I'm sure, but we're the friendly type with 'em. Let it be."

Nodding, I drop it and take a drink of the crisp, cool liquid. I'll be respectful to Scot, but damn sure believe I'll have my turn with Ares again. He's lucky I didn't take my hatchet to him like I do the others. I kept it clean, only fighting with my fists; the club should've stayed out of it.

No wonder they needed our help on that California problem if that's how they handle a little scrapping. *Bunch of pussies!*

Speaking of pussy, I could use some tonight and not the gash that was hanging around the clubhouse. Those bitches around there are a little too prim and proper for me. I need a naughty bitch, one who isn't scared of getting dirty as I fill her up.

Saint and Sinner take the seats on the other side of me, sitting back and relaxing.

"Where're you two coming from?" We all arrived here at the same time, but those two fuckers disappeared quickly.

Saint turns toward me, his light gray eyes meeting my gaze, with his full-on pretty boy looks. The man could be a fucking buff cover model for Abercrombie or some shit. Sinner looks similar, just the dark version, with his jet black hair and charcoal colored irises. I swear to God those fuckers are real brothers and don't know it.

"We wanted our cocks sucked." He shrugs and Sinner grins alongside him.

"Well fuck! I want my cock sucked too." Grumbling, I scan the room, instantly stopping on some sexy blonde bitch talking up one of the skinny Prospects from the Oath Keepers.

She's exactly what I need with those sultry lips, plump enough to wrap tightly around my dick and suck until her cheeks flush. I'd spray my load all over that flawless skin gracing her face.

Finishing the last of my drink, I stand and adjust myself; baby already has me getting full for her. Taking a deep eager breath, I swagger over toward the couple. Immediately turning toward the pissant Prospect, I snarl, "Thanks, newbie, but I'll take her from here."

Since when do Prospects chat up chicks? When I was prospecting, you shut the fuck up and were the last man on the totem pole to get any female attention.

His eyes grow wide, knowing he better back up, even though his forehead wrinkles in irritation. At least the cat's smart enough to keep his damn mouth shut.

I turn to the blonde, ready to show her I'm the better choice, only to find she's gone. Vanished like a goddamn ghost or some shit. Figures, she's the first one in a while that I want to stick my cock in, and she disappears.

"Where'd she go, Prospect?" I growl, and he shrugs.

"I don't know; I'd never seen her before. She was only in here a minute before you scared her off."

"The fuck you trying to say?"

"Nothin' man." He puts his hands up and takes a step closer to his Prospect buddy.

He's never going to get a full patch if he can't show some balls. The Oath Keepers would not let a weakling in full-time.

"You see her again, you send her to me. Got it?"

"Yep." He nods, and I take my seat again.

"No luck, brother?" Saint smirks.

Rolling my eyes, I ignore him and gesture so Nancy will bring me another drink. A small hand runs up my arms and a pair of big tits press up against my back. Hot breath hits my ear the same time as Saint and Sinner both break out in grins.

"You want your cock sucked, baby? Your friends sure liked it."

Glancing at my brothers, they nod, easily agreeing with her, so I stand and adjust my dick. My pants are still tight from the blonde so that I could use some relief. Twisting around, I find a mousy redhead with tits probably bigger than double Ds and a decent mouth.

"Let's go," I mutter as I catch her wrist and yank her toward the door. *Finally, time to get serviced.*

PRINCESS

I INHALE ANOTHER DRAG OFF THE CIGARETTE. MY FATHER would shit if he saw me smoking. I'm an adult, but my father's always treated me like I'm fifteen years old. So naturally that eggs me on even more to do shit that would piss him off. I know, real mature, but fuck him.

He made his choice long ago when he chose his club over his loved ones. I guess his real family wasn't good enough for him and his life, so he went and made his own. It wouldn't have been so bad if he'd included us in everything, but he kept my brother and me far away from it.

Then when I was younger, he was in jail for years because of his friends running drugs with him. What a loser. Being away from him for so long has been a blessing as far as I'm concerned.

Now, he suddenly wants to pull a stunt and show up at my mom's house all the time, like he fucking cares about her? Fuck that! He broke her so badly before. I'm older this time around, and I'm not letting him get away with it.

Hence the Prospect from the Oath Keepers I was just talking to—Scratch. I still can't believe he'd let people call him that, and frankly, I'm scared to find out how he got it.

At least I have a plan. Well, my best friend, Bethany, came up with it at first, but it's brilliant. I'm going to go from daddy's little good girl to his naughty biker slut, and I'm making sure it's personal for him. As soon as B mentioned it, I was sold.

Paybacks will come swift and easy for me by fucking a few of his club brothers. Surely they would love a young blonde with a perky rack and tight cunt. I could probably walk right through that club door and get picked up by a few of them.

Once I'm done sleeping with some of them and I can rub it in my father's face, I'll embarrass him in front of everyone. I'll figure out when he'll be around his oh so precious fucking club and announce it. I may even point out which of his men dipped into the honey jar. Once he's mortified and disrespected, I'll be out of there. It'll teach the bastard to fuck with my loved ones once and for all.

In the past, I'd have never had the guts or would've thought about this plan, but now he has my older brother, Brently, joining that stupid gang too. I refuse to let my mom lose Brently as well. She sacrificed her husband already, and it's not fair to take her son also.

My brother met me to have lunch last week; it was quick but better than nothing. *Nothing* has been the norm for him lately. He's been pulling no-shows and not returning any of our calls or texts. Then, I couldn't believe it at the diner when he showed up proudly wearing a cut that was just like my father's. The only big differences were that Brent's said 'Prospect' and 'Snake' for his name.

Seriously? Because the experience from the psychos who carved him up and attacked him wasn't bad enough already? The club members went ahead and chose a name off of it for him?

It sounds more like a slap in the face if you ask me. They're calling him that shit after what the attackers did to torment him and the love of his life. I don't get it how Brent can stand to be around them after that.

My brother felt like me for so long, never wanting anything to do with the club or our father. We both graduated with good grades and went to college. I was on the drill team in high school, and he stayed busy playing sports. We both made our mom so proud; she supported everything when it came to us.

I went to a junior college since my father wouldn't pay for a larger school, and I had to go where financial aid would allow. It was extra shitty because I remember him getting a new Harley that year. At least, in the end, it meant that I still had my mom and Bethany around me.

Brently, on the other hand, got to go away to a decent college. He was awarded a sports scholarship that paid most of his way. Not like any of it matters anymore, with his chosen career path. He's turned into a giant asshole just like my dad.

After all the lying and cheating my father put my mom through, I just can't forgive him. Now Brently's going on that list too. He should be helping me, not making it harder. *Traitor!*

I haven't spoken to my mom in almost four weeks. I kept seeing my dad's new bike parked out front of her house, so I didn't want to stop by. Then, he's answered her phone every time I've called, so I gave up ringing her.

When it comes down to it, I don't have anything to say to him right now. I'd rather keep driving or hang up, than waste more breath on being angry at him. Obviously, my words in the past never did anything to change his ways, so hopefully this drastic plan of mine will.

In the beginning, when he'd pull his shit with Mom, I'd been able to speak to her about it. She was always saying that she needed him, which I know was a load of bull. I've been the one around her—all the time—even when I was in college in Austin. She's always been such a strong woman; she never sees it, though. He breaks her over and over, yet she rebuilds herself.

Sure, there've been nights when I'd hear her crying or when he'd call lit off his ass begging to talk to her, but he never showed up every day like he's been doing. We'd go for little spurts of him being around for like three days, and then he'd vanish again. Each time he'd show up with the same sob story of 'he couldn't take it anymore, and he loved her.'

I never understood back then or now, how she could easily forgive him. Her favorite justification, when confronted about it, was always 'love's blind and forgiving.' Well, I'll embarrass him so badly this time that he'll stay away from my mom for good. She won't have to make excuses for him any longer. I never want my dad to hurt her ever again; she deserves real love and happiness.

He's done all that and yet the guys he has with him call him the Prez. What kind of shitty man like that deserves to be called the President of any organization?

Ugh. Maybe getting my payback will end up opening my brother's eyes again.

When I showed up at that crappy bar tonight, it was pure blind luck on my part. I stopped in to see if they knew where I could find some of the Oath Keepers guys. The bar's located near the clubhouse, so I figured I'd give it a shot. I struck freaking gold when—pretty much right away—I ran into one of their Prospects. He was cute and seemed kinda sweet, definitely looking to get laid until the big guy showed up to interrupt us.

The other man was insanely good-looking, but he was no Prospect. As soon as the wild group of bikers came barreling into the bar, my body went on guard. Their cuts said Nomad and my mother's warned me about those types of guys, as well as club members from back in her time with my father.

With the lifestyle they live, I seriously doubt I could handle one of them. But, I may try it out in the future, especially if it's with the guy I saw tonight. Sweet fucking baby Jesus that man was so delicious looking. He seemed rough and sexy all over, and to top it off; his name patch said 'Viking.'

It was the last thing I saw before I was headed out the door, needing to regroup and come up with a better game plan. Because fuck me, how on earth do you get called something like Viking? You know it can't just be because he's massive. It has to be more. I'm betting he's a very dangerous man, and the scary thing is, that sounds fucking hot.

Next week I'm damn sure dragging Bethany back in there with me to help. It was her idea originally, so she better be up on acting as my wingman. She'll probably flip out and offer to fuck them all. She's a total slut, but I still love her. I'm not the only one with daddy issues, but hers are far more fucked up than mine. The poor woman was beaten and molested by the man who helped create her. I don't know how she did it; I most likely would have stabbed him when he slept if it were me.

Also, some much-needed recon is due for the Prospect; any information on him at all would help me out. Oh and Viking too. But how? My mother wouldn't know either of them, not that I would get to speak to her anyhow. My dad's probably over at the house, and God knows I don't want to talk with him.

Not far from the bar, I pull into the parking lot of my quaint apartment. Climbing out of my car, I slam the door, relieved to be home.

It's nothing special, but it's become home to me and occasionally Bethany when she decides to stay over. I don't make a lot of money, but it's enough to get me by, thankfully. I've never been one for many material things, even with a name like Princess hung over me.

Tossing my clothes in my hamper, I sluggishly make my way to my awesome fluffy bed and face-plant. I'm buzzed and exhausted. It's the perfect way to end my day, with a good night's sleep.

Two

PRINCESS

The next night...

AS I'M GETTING DRESSED, MY PHONE GOES OFF, FLASHING Bethany's name across the screen,

"What's up, chick?" I mutter into the phone as soon as I hit *accept*, propping it on my shoulder and pull on a sock.

"You have to get over here," she shouts loudly over the blaring music in the background.

"Where are you exactly?" A party or a bar, that's for sure.

"I'm at a Coop's place. You remember Cooper from eleventh grade?"

"Cooper Williams?" I guess, squinting my eyes as I picture him and Polo shirts from years back. He was somewhat popular back when we were in high school. Nice guy, but nothing special to me.

"Yeah! He's back and having a party, but that's not why I called you."

"Okaaay." I bite my lip waiting; she doesn't sound bombed yet, but she's on that route.

"There's a guy here! And, he's wearing a Prospect cut from your dad's gang. His name is Stitch or Scratch, or, umm...I don't know, something like that. Anyhow, get over here!"

"That's the same guy I met last night at the bar." *Scratch.* Thinking of him instantly has my mind flashing to Viking.

"I saw the text you sent me this morning about meeting a Prospect; that's why as soon as I saw the guy's name, I called you. Is he the one?"

"Thanks, and yeah, I believe it is. I have to do my makeup and can be there in like an hour."

"What if he leaves? You need to come here now, this your chance."

"Okay, I'll try to hurry. Does Cooper still live in the same house as high school?"

"Yeah, same place."

"Okay cool, see you soon."

"Bye, bitch!" she shouts, laughing, and I hang up.

Lucky for me, Cooper had a ton of get-togethers in high school, so everyone from this area knows where he lives. I'm not looking forward to seeing that crowd; I'm sure it'll be littered with floozies, but oh well. This is about my plan, not partying.

Instead of taking my time getting ready as I would prefer, I lose the comfy socks and shimmy into my favorite pair of daisy dukes. I quickly slide on my new summer sandals, because they pair up perfectly. I look cute but casual. To top my outfit off and make it pop a little, I line my eyes with black kohl and brush on some bright pink lipstick. Men say they hate lipstick, but they love that shit, especially if it's smeared a little by them.

Thank God my hair's already dry, or it'd set me back another twenty minutes. The blonde locks damn near brush my waist, just like my mom's always have.

I stuff my ID and some cash in my back pocket, grab my phone and keys and then I'm on my way. The drive takes about fifteen minutes, and as soon as I park, I'm jumping out of my car. I can tell myself all I want that I'm in a rush to see if my dad's Prospect is still here, but even I know that's bullshit. Viking's who I want to catch a glimpse of.

Bethany's easy for me to spot as I find her playing beer pong—her usual—so I make my way over. Pinching her butt, I step to the side, messing with her a little, and she turns—surprised—until she realizes it's me. I get instantly embraced in an exaggerated hug and giggle, so she's been drinking awhile.

"Damn, that was fast." She smiles.

"I hurried. I want a beer and to see this guy again."

"Okay, come on, there's still liquor left too if you want a few shots." She pokes her beer pong partner's arm until he gives her some attention. "Play my turn; I'll be right back."

"You promise?" He slurs like the typical weak frat boy out of his neighborhood, causing me to roll my eyes. Another loser seems like, already pretty plastered and guaranteed to puke at some point.

"Be right back." She nods to him and yanks my wrist, so I follow her toward the kitchen.

"Who's the dude?" I gesture back to Mr. Beer Pong.

"I don't know," she laughs, "but he's kinda' cute."

"You could do better; he has *puker* written all over him," I argue.

"I'm not picky." She shrugs and I keep my mouth shut, grabbing a beer from a bald guy manning the keg.

"Thanks," I say, tipping my cup toward him slightly since he didn't fill it to the top and have it spill everywhere. The guy obviously knows how to pour a beer.

"Anytime," he smirks looking me up and down like I'm his next conquest.

Ugh, go polish your forehead, douche.

Bethany leads me back to the beer pong table so she can keep playing and the beat kicks up to one of my favorite songs by The Hills. The volume gets cranked even louder after a second in what should be the living room. The new song pouring through the oversized speakers draws my attention to the people dancing, and I spot the Prospect. He's leaning against the living room wall, just watching them all.

Scratch's giving me such an easy in right now, and he doesn't even know it. Swaying my hips like I want to dance, I make my way over into his direct line of sight. My gaze hits his briefly, just enough to draw him to me, as I grind my hips seductively to the beat.

Like bees to honey, he's on me in no time at all. Just like that, he's already hooked; I know it. He pulls my waist into him, gripping my hips securely. Following my rhythm, he moves along with me at first, eventually taking over the lead.

My red solo cup gets crunched, and beer starts to spill over, so I take a few big gulps and attempt to concentrate on not spilling it down my chin as well, while we continue to dance. I'd appreciate it if I could get some sort of buzz established; it'd give me a boost of courage to do what I need to later.

I wasn't the type who went out and fucked around in high school. I wouldn't be labeled as a good girl per se, but I wasn't a whore by any extent. College was different; I explored some and had a good time, but most of all, I learned what I liked. This situation, though, is slightly nerve racking. I'm planning to seduce Scratch when I don't want him. Like at all.

As soon as the red cup leaves my lips, he reaches around and takes it from me. Before I can get turned around to protest, he finishes the liquid off and tosses the plastic cup toward an overfull trash can.

"I wanted more," I state loudly and cock my eyebrow. I *needed* it.

Grinning playfully, Scratch tugs my front into him, until our faces are so close that our noses are almost brushing together. He takes the lead again as our bodies gyrate against each other, and his leg pushes between mine. His firm palms cup my ass, applying enough pressure so that each time he moves, my pussy rubs against his thigh and gets a little wetter. We're close enough that I can easily feel his cock hardening with each thrust.

"We can get more later," he says watching my eyes and mouth each time he presses me against his thigh. Giving him the reaction he craves, I imagine riding the big biker's thigh from the other night and part my lips letting a small, breathy moan escape, building up his ego.

Scratch's fairly good-looking with his fuller lips, hazel eyes, and shaved short hair. By the dancing, he doesn't appear to be in bad shape either. He's slightly more on the thinner side than what I normally would be attracted to, but this isn't about me finding a man and my preferences. It's strictly based on my mission to fuck with my dad and his club.

Running my hands over his back, I pierce my nails into his

shoulders coercing Scratch to me so he thinks that I can't possibly get enough of him. He complies, feathering his lips over my neck, pressing wet kisses as he goes.

I need to clear my mind and get into it; I have to make this happen. I want to get it over with as soon as possible, so I'm going to make this nice and simple for him.

"Do you want to go somewhere with some privacy?" I suggest breathily next to his ear.

"Yeah, sugar, I'm cool with whatever."

Bingo.

Thank God he has no idea who I am, because if so, he'd also know that my father would strangle him for kissing all over me like he is. Not having a good relationship with my dad doesn't mean he wouldn't teach his Prospect a lesson. It'd take a certain kind of man for the Prez not to scare the shit out of them.

Thinking about it, makes me giddy inside. It's so fucked up, but I can't stop feeling this way, knowing I'll be one step closer to sleeping with a few of them. Then I'll get to break it to my father that his club has benefitted me as well. I'll finally get that small piece of satisfaction knowing I've hurt and disappointed my dad like he's done to my poor mom for so long. In the end, she'll be happier with him gone, and that's all I want.

Payback's a bitch, motherfucker.

"Great, let's see if we can find a room or something."

"Even better." He nods, following me down Cooper's narrow hallway until we find an empty bedroom. I should have brought a leash; it's been that easy so far.

Once I'm over the threshold and pulling Scratch inside the room with me, I kick the door closed. Ready to make this real for him and get my head in the game, I begin kissing him passionately. Closing my eyes, I search for my happy place. I'll be pushing it all to the back of my mind as soon as possible anyhow. I need to make this memorable for him. I want him to brag as much as possible, especially around the clubhouse. Then once it comes out to my dad, everyone will know about it already.

Scratch instantly reciprocates, his hands eagerly wandering all over my body. He rushes the entire process like he's going to burst in his pants. I was expecting his hands to be callused since he's a wannabe biker and all, but they're soft.

Why does that seem so wrong to me? Have I ever noticed callused hands before? Maybe it's because I would assume him being rough and tough, but I'm not even naked yet, and he's not meeting my expectations.

Shit! Fuck! What expectations? Erase them, bury that crap, and stick to your plan.

He pulls away breathing heavier, pushing his groin into me a few times. Scratch's so wound up; he starts kissing over my throat again as he pants, "Let me get you off first in case I don't last. You're one fine piece of ass, sugar; you ever been with a biker before?"

"No, and I don't want to talk about it either." God, no talking or his breath may kill me. Hot beer scent isn't something that excites my pussy. "I think the cut is hot, though." I throw in for extra measure like he's going to be some prize for me, hopefully building up his ego. "Please, I want you so badly, I can't help myself. I can't believe I saw you here; it must have been meant to be."

It all sounds so rehearsed and fake. *Because it is.*

If I don't work on this better and end up getting an experienced club guy, he'll be able to see right through me. My entire plan could be blown to shit, everything going downhill if that happens. Or else next time I need to make sure I've had a few shots or something, and then I'd be able to blur it all and relax.

"Well I wouldn't go that far, but us havin' fun was meant to be, for sure," he mumbles on his way to my chest.

I get tired of him slobbering on me so I push him off, his eyes meeting mine, confused. The first dirty thought stumbles out to get him back on track. "I can think of better places for that tongue."

"Fuck yeah, that's what I'm talking about."

"Okay, over here."

"Perfect," Scratch says and catches my arms, pulling me to him. He guides me, walking backward as we're pressed up against each other. His body is warming me with each step until the pits of my knees hit the mattress. The bed's made up with a hunter green duvet and appears to still be clean. Thankfully, I don't think anyone's found their way in here yet. Regardless, I'm not touching the sheets, so I'll just lie on top.

He pushes my shorts down my legs, his hand shooting between my thighs excitedly. I use the alcohol and my determination to get my body turned on, wetting his overzealous hand.

I feel like a fucking whore right now. Tons of women would be stoked to be here with him; he's decent, just not for me. Time to fucking suck it up and do this to hurt my father. I'll wound him any way possible to pay him back for the heartache and distress he's caused our family, even if I have to play the bad guy for a little while. I want him to feel such disappointment and embarrassment, just as I have my entire life growing up. I want his fucking heart to hurt. Empty inside from the father that was never there.

"I thought I was getting your mouth?" I don't want to fuck him, so if I can get away with oral that would surely count toward my goal. No doubt he'll be back at the clubhouse bragging about how he had some blonde chick on her knees the night prior.

"You can have whatever you want with that tight little puss you got down there. I can't wait to taste you, sugar" he mumbles and squats.

His fingers leave my wetness and tangle in the strings of my underwear as he carelessly pulls on them, yanking the elastic toward him. I don't know if he thought he could rip them or what, but it doesn't work so he shoves them down to my ankles. He leaves them resting at my feet and pushes his face between my legs.

Scratch's nose bumps my clit instantly, causing my center to clench up in a jolt of pleasure. No way am I going to be able to do this standing up; it'll feel way too good if he has any clue whatsoever as to what he's doing. He seems rushed, but he zeroed in on my sensitive spot with the first shot, so this could end up not being so bad.

Sitting, I scoot back toward the pillows, making sure to leave enough room for him to climb on the bed also. As he follows my body to the mattress, he pushes my legs wide open. His soft hands run along my thighs, parting them as far as possible, giving him a full view of my pink center.

Scratch leans in, giving my pussy long powerful strokes with his tongue. Each enticing lick's being accompanied by skilled fingers relentlessly plunging in and out of my tight entrance. It seems like no time passes as my head's thrown back, moaning out my pleasure, riding the wave as it starts to hit me and make the entire world disappear.

Holy shit! Maybe I should fuck him after all.

I'm beyond surprised with his persistence as my hips thrust into his face, twisting and jerking as I work my way up to my release. My fingers rake through his short hair as I pull his mouth into me as much as I can to ride his tongue through my orgasm.

Once I'm depleted, I'm left panting and wide-eyed. Not often can a man eat pussy like that, and fuck if he isn't one of the best I've had in a long time. Maybe this mission of mine won't be such a bad thing after all. God, if the Prospect's that good, I can only imagine how Viking would be. I'd probably fucking die.

"Fuck, you got a greedy pussy."

I can't think of a reply; he's completely right. I let loose a low giggle, and he shoots me a goofy smile.

"What's your name, sugar?"

So now he's curious? Typical man, waiting until the panties are off for formalities. "Princess."

He thinks about it a minute, before repeating me. "Princess? That's your actual name? Kinda fits after I've tasted ya."

"Yep, my daddy said he knew that he'd be Prez one day, so they went ahead and named me Princess."

His eyes widen, and he swallows down a cough that's suddenly bubbled up. His face becomes sour as he thinks hard, his forehead wrinkling with tension.

Continuing on, it all comes out almost like a taunt. "You know, of the Oath Keepers? You're wearing the cut, so surely you'd know that you had your fingers and tongue all up inside his daughter." I feel like such a bitch giving him a snotty answer, but fuck it; I have to be one to drive my point in.

"Fuck...I'm dead! They'll fucking kill me for this!"

"No. Lucky for you, he doesn't care about his family, so you have nothing to worry about. If anything, now you have bragging rights to the brothers. You are, after all, the very first one who's touched me out of them."

"Oh, God, I'm really fuckin' dead now. I gotta go." Standing suddenly, he straightens out his clothes, wiping the sweat off that's suddenly on his brow with the back of his hand.

"But I thought you wanted to fuck? Or you wanted me to return the favor with my mouth?" Licking my lips, I smile devilishly, and I swear he whimpers.

Taking a step closer toward the door, he chuckles weakly. "God, you're gorgeous, but I'm trying to stay alive. If I fuck you, then I'd be signing my death certificate. Ares, our VP would chop me into little pieces. We all know if he wouldn't have claimed his Ol' Lady, then the Prez would want his VP with his daughter. It's like some unspoken rule in biker clubs. I have to go before the wrong person notices that I'm with you." Shaking his head apologetically, he's out the door in a flash. I don't even have time to get any argument out.

In his wake, I hit the mattress as I fall backward, bouncing and then slamming my fists onto the bed, irritated.

Damn it. He's so freaked out; I don't think he'll open his mouth about it. *Ugh.* What should I do? I don't think there's much I can do, besides put his name on my list and move onto another.

Surely there has to be one of them that will gloat about it and not be too scared. Hell, Scratch is a man; he'll have to open his mouth to someone. Men always brag about their conquests.

If anything, one day I may have to head over to the clubhouse when I'm certain that my father's not around. Ares knows what I look like, but most of them haven't seen me since I was a little girl. I'd be able to scope out the brothers and see if Scratch brags when the guys say something about me because they will. I'll make sure to wear something that easily gets their attention.

Sitting up, I pat my hair, smoothing the frazzled mess and collect myself for a moment. Scooting to the edge of the bed, I find my panties and tug them back on, and then stand to adjust my shorts. Inhaling a deep breath, I nod, satisfied with my orgasm and plan I've decided on. It'll work; I have to stay persistent.

Oath Keepers members were crawling all over that little bar I went to. I'll find another. Until then, my ass is going home to shower, sleep, and regroup some more. Scratch was a nice guy, but not my forever type. I want to get home to scrub the memories off as soon as possible.

VIKING

Four days later...

SITTING AT THE SMALL ROUND TABLE IN FRONT OF THE crappy hotel window, I watch across the street as Saint and Sinner leave with yet another new woman from that shitty little bar we've been going to. I don't know where these bitches come from; it seems like they multiply each night that we're there.

I'm not complaining; having my cock sucked regularly has been pretty fucking nice. It'd be even better if I found someone worth fuckin' though. The women available have been run through time and again. They serve their purpose when it comes to pleasing ya, but I'm not trying to stick my dick in one and have a bitch fall in love or some dumb shit.

The truth is, I've shown up every single night hoping to catch that sexy ass blonde chick I saw the first time my brothers, and I stopped in. We had come straight over after we handled some business for the MC. It was Saturday night, and she hasn't been back since; even the bartender confirmed that she hadn't seen her either.

I'm wondering if maybe 'cause it was the weekend? Regardless, I can't shake that mouth and those tits from my mind. I go to sleep thinking about them and wake up hard as fuck. I can only imagine what she'd feel like wrapped around me, hot and wet, her little cunt throbbing as I make her come.

She could be a college chick, maybe looking to play with some bad boys to get her kicks or some shit. Wouldn't surprise me, it's happened before. I have no problem whatsoever showing her just what a real fuckin' bad boy is.

I'd fuck her twenty ways to Sunday. She'd be begging me to stop 'cause she wouldn't be able to stand up anymore. That's what a real man would do with a piece of ass like hers.

Turned on again, I unclasp the button on my jeans and reach inside to start pumping my thick cock. Giving it an extra tight squeeze, I picture her tightness clasping down, grinding, while I made her scream.

Fuck! I groan, full of need. Pumping a few times, my thoughts switch to her tits bouncing while she rides me. My sac keeps tightening more and more, my balls ready to explode.

Pulling my eyes away from my throbbing length, a near silent gasp escapes my mouth as I watch a platinum blonde's ass in a short black skirt. She sashays across the gravel parking lot; her arm looped through another chick's, and the sight of her hips swinging has warm jets of my seed splashing onto my shirt.

The sun's setting so I can just make out everything perfectly, and I'd bet fifty bucks it's the bitch I was just dreaming of. Like a freshman excited for his first fuck, I jump from my chair. Pulling my jeans closed, I stuff my wallet in my back pocket.

Most of the guys are already over there, so I'll join them until I'm able to make certain it's her. Better get over there quick before someone else attempts to get in her pants like that fucking Prospect from last weekend. I wanted to beat his ass so badly after she disappeared but held myself back. My brothers seem to like this bar for some reason, so I'm trying to keep the peace.

Saint and Sinner have been in their room mere minutes when I head outside and can already hear the chick they had with them moaning loudly. Her long wails remind me of a cat in heat, maybe the rest of us will get lucky too, and they'll gag the bitch. It's not often they go off with someone alone. One would think they'd get tired of sharing all the time, I damn sure couldn't handle that shit.

The highway's never busy, so I amble on across and make my way through the pebbled gravel parking lot. Headed toward the entry, my gaze settles on a shiny group of bikes parked out front. My curiosity's peaked because none of them belong to the Nomads or the other regulars that've been here all week.

They'll be straight as long as they stay the fuck out of my way.

The music from the jukebox pours outside as I head through the entrance and spot my brothers. Tucked back in the corner, they all sit facing the majority of the room. One thing about these guys, even if they've been drinking all day, they'll keep their guards up. The Nomads stay ready in case shit goes south. Never knew a group like that before and had come to appreciate them. It makes a hell of a difference knowing someone else has your six.

Scot nods hello as I make my way over to them. As I return it, Spider's fist pops out in front of me so I can bump knuckles with him. "'Sup, Vike?"

"Spidey."

Damn sure could use a drink; I sound like I just woke up.

"Brother." Nightmare nods in acknowledgment as I sit near him at the high top.

"Figured it was time for a cold one." I'm here to check out a female. Not that I plan on alerting them or the fucking media to it, though. Keeping her to me will be tricky, but I'll figure it out. None of these fuckers need a sample; that's for damn sure.

Stacy, a part-time bar girl, sets a glass bottle down in front of me. It's chilled enough that the amber colored glass is foggy, letting me know that she listened to me and grabbed it from the bottom of the beer cooler.

Taking the first sip, the alcohol hits my tongue like a burst of refreshing, icy bliss. *God, I love it when bitches listen to me, and a good, cold beer.*

"Would you like anything else to drink, Viking?" She cuts straight to it. Stacy doesn't try the bullshit flirting or anything like that. Setting her straight on day one, I let her know that I'm not some ass clown in here she can fool. Since then, we've been cool, and I tip her better. Like tonight, this beer just got her a kick-ass tip.

"Nope, I'm good. How's your night so far?"

"Same as always." She smiles, and I nod. "If you decide to change it up, let me know."

Handing her a five, she attempts to give me my change, but I ignore it. She smiles and then takes off back toward the bar.

Once Stacy's out of my line of sight, my eyes search *her* out. My gaze meets *hers,* and it hits me that she was already staring at me. I'm betting that she watched me from the moment I walked through the door.

Is she just checking me out? Or could she be jealous that Stacy was over here smiling? Nah, she's way too happy right now to be the bitter type. She and the little friend she's here with are playing a game of pool, giggling and drinking what looks like their second beer already.

Glancing around, I find that damn near every other motherfucker in the place is watching them as well. I haven't even sampled her yet, and she already has my adrenaline spiking. I can't remember a time when a chick has had my body humming like this, and especially it being from someone peeping on her.

A few scrawny bastards whistle as hot chick bends over to make her shot and my insides stir something fierce. My hands tingle, feeling like I could break a fool's fingers one by one for touching her.

I don't know if it's 'cause I haven't fucked in a whole minute or what, but she's got my dick wanting to stand loud and proud under this damn table. That's the last thing I want my brothers popping off, giving me shit for right now. I'm going to let her have some fun with her friend for a little while before making a move. She'll get a couple more drinks in her and probably loosen up some so she won't bolt again when I speak to her.

Sipping my beers, the night drags on with me sitting quietly, attempting to learn everything about her from afar. My brothers start to notice my unusual drinking activity and eventually realize I'm not paying them any attention, but instead, giving it all to her. I can't stop either.

The way her calves flex when she walks around the pool table in her sky-high shoes, makes me want to grab her wrists one handed, behind her back and bend her over. Then her long silky hair brushes the top of her ass every time she moves. It's fucking taunting me, waiting for me to wrap it around my fist and pull it. Sweetheart has no idea the type of hell I'd put her through, to bring her pleasure.

Taking another swallow of beer, I imagine yet another way I'd have her. This time, she'd be on her knees, cheeks flushed and begging me to let her swallow my cum. Letting loose a growl at the image, my brothers turn to me, eyebrows cocked.

Nightmare hikes his lip up slightly, almost in a grin, but not completely. He doesn't ever really smirk or smile. "Talk to her."

Scot chuckles. "Aye laddie, the lass would probably love a good ride." I shoot him a glare just as the hot chick shouts to her friend that she's going to go out for a quick smoke. She glances at me briefly as she's declaring it, almost like an invitation.

She saunters closer to our table and as she does, her lashes lower, and her lip slightly pouts. I already wanted that luscious mouth the first time I saw her. With that bottom lip out a bit, it's doing fucking insane things to the rock hard cock in my jeans.

She checks me out from head to toe the entire time that she passes us. Swinging those hips a little too much, knowing damn well that she has every brother's attention at our table. It's so goddamn seductive and obvious; it hits me that it's no innocent invitation. It's a fucking dare. She doesn't think I'll actually go out there. *Challenge accepted.*

Like a dumbass, she strolls down the hallway toward the bathrooms. No doubt that she's going out the back door to have a smoke all alone. Doesn't she have any means of self-preservation? She can't announce that shit and then amble on out alone.

Some guy posted up against the wall near the same hall, follows her, easily catching up. I watch as the idiot smiles all friendly-like and holds the door for her. It's probably a good time to have my own smoke. I hadn't seen him out in the bar, so I have no clue who the fuck he is.

"I'mma smoke." Grumbling, I stand and think of squirrels in pink tutus to get my dick to go soft. The brothers nod, continuing with their conversation that I wasn't paying any mind to.

Stopping along the way, the alcohol's set in so I take a piss. Then head outside as well.

The door closes, engulfing the classic rock, leaving me in the quiet, humid night. Leaning against the building, I fish my cigarettes out of my front jeans pocket, shaking them so one pops out enough that I can put it straight to my lips. Shoving the packet back into my pocket, I dig my fingers around until they find my Zippo, and it comes out next.

Flipping the top open, I flick it, so the bright orange and blue flame comes to life as I cup my other hand around it, lighting my cigarette. Closing the lid, I stuff the non-descript metal Zippo back in my pocket and inhale a long, relieving drag, just as I hear the first low whimper.

Holding my breath and remaining still, my gaze starts to scan over everything around me. Nothing pops out, but I know what I heard. There's a small brick building about twelve paces away, most likely for the bar storage. A dim light hangs from behind the poorly built structure, not doing much to illuminate the area.

A pained cry comes next, louder, echoed by another; this one tainted with anger. Off to the side of the storage, it's shadowed, but I'm able to make out what looks to be a struggle happening.

Launching off the small porch, I bring the cigarette to my lips and inhale another deep drag before tossing it off into the gravel. With large, quick strides, I make my way over to the shadowed area. Remaining as quiet as possible, I creep the last few paces to get a good look at what's going on. It could be a wild fuck for all I know, or it could be someone getting attacked.

The shady looking guy from the hallway has the blonde shoved up against the brick, ripping at her clothes. She's not giving it freely, but fighting for her fucking life, pounding her petite fists into him over and over. He slams her into the building, frustrated, going for her lacey bra next and she emits a wounded whimper from impact, the sound stabbing into my soul.

Consumed by his dick, shady fuck hisses, "I've watched those bikers show up and take all the women around here, well not you. I'm fucking you, no matter if I have to kill you first or not."

Her hands fly toward his face, attempting to shove him away. "Get off of me you piece of shit!" she cries.

The rage inside grows, overtaking and overwhelming any bit of self-control that I once possessed. My body vibrates as I'm unable to hold myself back any longer, nor do I want to. Blood rushes through my body, my veins pumping full as the adrenaline hits me full force, wanting to explode. Deep red, the color of blood, begins to cloud my vision from witnessing someone physically hurt her like this, to hear the fear and helplessness in her sweet voice.

"She said no, motherfucker," I rasp, angrily. It takes so much to utter those simple words and not just rip him from her, but I don't want to frighten her more by slaughtering him in front of her.

He turns toward me with a snarl painted on his lips, but I give him no time to react. Eagerly wrapping my hand around his throat, I lift him completely off the ground. Thrusting him forward, I beat his skull into the wall. His head emits a loud smack sound each time it crashes against the rough brick, totaling three times.

It dazes shady fuck enough for me to glance toward the shaken woman. Her red lipstick's all over her mouth and chin, her mascara smeared down her cheeks from her tears, dirtying her up a bit. I've never seen a woman more beautiful before.

Her gratitude-filled blue eyes meet mine like I'm some sort of fucking hero or a saint. As the wetness continues to trail over her cheeks, it ignites an entirely different creature. The urge to breed—to *fuck* her into submission—grows rampant. The animal wanting to claw it's way free and take over what this shady fuck was about to do.

I never said I was a decent man. Upstanding citizen hasn't ever fit in my description. There are these thoughts I have; it doesn't mean

I've acted on them before. But fuck if it isn't the strongest right now, wanting to take this bitch and ride her hard.

The asshole starts to squirm, my grip slipping slightly and stealing me out of the spell. "Go," I grunt and tighten my hold.

"O-okay." She swallows, pulling her shirt front together attempting to hide her bra, from where the douche ripped it completely open.

Her tall heels are forgotten as she takes off in a sprint toward the front of the building. Fumbling along the way, she calls someone, continuing to run. Probably her friend, to let her know what happened.

Shady fuck moves again, and I release my grip. He falls, stumbling to catch his balance as I plant a powerful punch to his gut, causing him to gasp for air.

"Who the fuck are you?" Stomping my heavy boot into his foot, I grind my heel down, planting him in place.

"Fuck you Oath Keeper!" he replies stubbornly.

I've always been an impatient man, hitting first and asking questions later. This idiot got a courtesy and didn't even realize it. My curiosity wanted answers, but my need for punishment wins out.

Pulling the small hatchet from my belt, I let loose a dark chuckle at what I'm about to do. I wanted to laugh when I was hitting him against the wall, but I would've terrified the beauty. Without another thought, I flash a grin and impale the blade of my ax into the top of his skull. It's not an easy feat, but I've had many times to practice throughout the years, and not to mention my size.

The brother's call me Viking for a reason, with my thighs resembling small tree trunks and my arms massive enough to make grown men cringe. My height easily dwarfs the average man; hell, I even tend to make the bigger ones look feeble when standing near me—if they have the guts to get that close in the first place. Usually, if the size doesn't scare them, then it's the Nordic Viking tattoos all over my body and the hatchet I keep on me.

There's a large gasp on impact, and my gaze flies to his expression. His eyes widen in shock, his mouth gaping in a horrific, tortured scream as I use both hands to wiggle the conveniently sized ax back out. It's wedged snuggly into the hard shell of his skull and takes some plying to remove. My favorite part's when they scream like this. Their eyes always widen with terror and disbelief that I'm going to kill them, and it's going to be painful.

Once the blade's free, he becomes motionless, staring like he's in a trance and I bring the hatchet down again. This time, the sharp object reaches far enough into the brain to do the damage I was craving. The man's once evil gaze glosses over as he falls to the ground, his life finished.

My dick hardens further as the rush of adrenaline sets in with the fact that I just killed for her. *She's mine.* My body hums in triumph.

With that one thought, I know I'd do it again. I'd kill for her as many times needed, no matter the reason. There's something about her that speaks to my darkness. It's fucking with my mind; I know absolutely nothing about her.

Hearing the bar door, I turn from the shady fucker and notice the chick's black heels she'd left behind in her haste. The light hits the shoes just enough to pick up the glossy texture and make them shine. They stand out like that stupid fairytale the girls in grade school used to talk about. Only I'm no Prince Charming, more like the big, bad wolf ready for dinner.

"Vike?" Spider rounds the corner, flicking a glance at the dead guy on the ground then to me. He watches as I place my hatchet into its holster on my leather belt. "You need some help dumping the body?"

"Appreciate it, brother," I reply, and he fist-bumps me.

This is a prime example of why I'm a part of this crew; they always have your back no matter the situation. There's not a bunch of bullshit questions or accusations, and the best part of all, they're all pretty fucked up in the head just like me.

"You wanna bury or burn it?"

There's a river not too far away, so I have a different idea that may not gain us attention or make us get all tired and filthy from digging. The only way I'd get dirty tonight would be if a sexy Cinderella were involved.

"Do you still have that container of liquid acid in your saddlebag?"

"Yeah. Fuck, you're gonna melt him?"

"I'm thinking we could pour some over his face and head where I hit him, and then dump the body in that river back there." I gesture into the darkness toward the sounds of rushing water.

Texas got so much rain this past week that it's been causing major flooding. The river here is up seven feet so far and still rising; authorities and weathermen are calling for everyone to stay away for fear of injuries and drownings. They've even closed some of the lakes as well. I'm betting it's the perfect scenario to dump a body easily. I could probably dump a dozen before anyone noticed.

"Good idea. I'll get it real quick." He takes off in a rush toward the front parking lot where his bike's located.

I'm drawn back to the shoes. Bending, I pick them up and inspect them closer. *Her calves in these were utterly fucking sinful.*

They look tiny in my hands and Cinderella's no small woman. I'd guess her to be around five foot eight or a little taller, but her shoes still look petite. There's nothing significant about the heels or on them to help me figure out who she could be.

Bringing them to my nose, I inhale, wanting some hint of her scent. I'm pleasantly surprised to find that they smell flowery. I'm guessing she must've put lotion on her feet before wearing them tonight.

I take another deep sniff like some psycho stalker, but I couldn't be fucked about that. She smells good—edible. This is the scent I would most likely incur as I ran my tongue up her calves, biting into the muscle tenderly while reveling in her smooth skin. You know it has to be soft; bitches like that always feel like they're an entirely different breed than the rest of us.

Spider hurries back; his chains secured to his wallet jingling with each step as he carefully carries the container. He peers over at the shoes I'm clutching for a moment, confused, but keeps his questions about them to himself.

"You want me to grab one of his legs so we can drag him?" His gesture doesn't go unnoticed. I know he only offered so I wouldn't have to put down the woman's heels and I won't forget it the next time he needs a brother to back him on something. Little shit like that goes a long way with me.

"Appreciate it, brother." I nod, carefully holding the pumps to my body and grab the right leg of the dead man.

Spider lifts the left ankle, holding the acid with his other hand as we set about dragging him in the dark toward the sounds of the river. He's fairly easy to move, save for him occasionally getting hung up on small bushes and what not. We both take careful strides; you never know where a snake hole or a dip may be, and I'm not trying to carry Spider's ass back 'cause he rolled his ankle not paying attention.

The aroma of rich topsoil grows stronger as we near the river's edge. The odor eventually becomes murkier—like muddy rainwater as we arrive at the bank.

We each drop the dead weight. Spider cautiously opens the acid, handing the container to me.

"Wait," he grumbles, pulling his cell phone out. The screen illuminates as he taps on it a few times. Eventually, a bright light shines out of it. "Flashlight app." He grins, pleased with himself.

"Nice."

Stepping toward the dude's head, but not too close, I tip the acid all over his face and the top of his skull where I had chopped a nice sized hole in it with my ax.

"Is it working?"

"I don't know. You sure do talk a lot when we're attempting to quietly dispose of a body, though."

"We're usually riding or drinking. Can't do much talking when there's a loud engine or music blaring."

"It's weird."

"I don't like the quiet."

Shrugging, I hand him the acid and the shoes.

I'm not checking if the guy's face is melted off; it's an image I can live without. I've gotten used to the blood and broken bones over the years, but I've never seen anyone melted before. The toxic smell floating in the air is enough to tell me not to look.

Not wanting to get any of that shit on me in case it really does burn your skin off, I turn the shady fuck over on his side and lift him, so his back is facing me. Inhaling a deep breath of burnt skin and damp earth, I powerfully toss his body out in front of me, biting my lip until I hear the splash of him hitting the water.

Spider shines his phone light over the water in front of us, and then along the banks. Either it's too dark, and we aren't seeing him, or the body landed in a good spot and is busy floating away.

"I need a beer," he mumbles after a beat.

"Fuck beer; I want whiskey." I need a sexy-ass blonde who wears super high black heels also, but I leave that part out.

Taking the shoes from him, we make the short trek back to the bar.

Four

PRINCESS

"I HAVE TO GO BACK TOMORROW," I DECLARE, GLANCING over at Bethany.

Her mouth gapes and she shakes her head. "Are you crazy, Prissy? No way! You were just attacked!"

She's called me Prissy for years. It only comes out when she's worried about something, though.

"Look, I know I was upset…"

"That's one hell of an understatement; seriously, think about what you're saying."

"I told you, that guy saved me. He didn't try anything either, just stopped that creep from hurting me further."

"How do you know the jerkoff who hurt you won't be there when you go back?"

"I just do."

"You're so full of shit."

"I saw the big guy hit him, and then when I was running away, there was a loud wail. I don't think the biker made it easy on him."

In fact, I know he didn't. Once I was far enough away, I had glanced back and seen him hit my attacker with something that wasn't his fist. The outline from the weak lighting made it look like a scene out of a horror movie.

The fucked up part about it all is that I'm not frightened. If anything, I'm curious. I want to go and see what he did to the bastard, see if he killed him.

I've never had anyone convey that type of violence for me before. Being so terrified and then witnessing that same feeling wash over my attacker was exhilarating. My savior didn't scare me one bit; he empowered me.

I'll never be some biker bitch or approve of my father's ways, but deep down, I know his blood runs through my veins. Pair it along with my mother's and it's no wonder I'm suddenly craving an outlaw. *I need to see him.*

He'd watched me all night. I could feel his blistering gaze on my back; it had taken every ounce of self-control I possessed not to look back and meet him head on. I don't think he's used to aggressive women and at first, I was on a mission to add him to my list. Now though…well, I have no idea what to do, but like a moth to a flame, all I can think about is getting back to him as quickly as possible.

"I still don't like it. I think you should stay away from that bar; your father's MC has a ton of other guys you can go for. Look, I get it; you're used to being a badass around normal people, but Princess, these guys aren't everyday people. You're a little woman compared to them, and if you go in there alone, they could kidnap you or something crazy and I'm betting no one would bat an eye."

Huffing, I count to five, so I keep my calm. *Wait, why am I getting upset over her talking down about those bikers anyhow? I hate them just as much, if not more.*

"You forget, Bethany, that my father's in charge of them. Besides, I won't be alone. You're coming with me."

"It's been two hours since I had to drive my best friend home because she was attacked and too upset to drive, and now she's sitting here, planning to drag me back to the place where it all went down? No way, cuz."

"Yes, that's right, I am your best friend, and I need a wingman. And for the record, stop with the cuz and cousin shit; people are going to think we're related, and I don't kiss my cousins!"

"Fine, but I'm not fucking one of them," she replies, her nose going up in the air like she's calling all the shots.

Yeah, okay, I won't hold my breath on that one. Those guys have her name written all over them. My snort pops out before I can hold it back.

She shoots me a heated glare, irritated.

I shrug, not saying anything and after a few moments her frown changes into an evil grin.

"Shut-up, I'm not going to sleep with them," she mumbles, and I outright laugh.

"Want to put some money on it?"

"No."

"'Cause you know I'm right."

"Whatever. I'm sleeping in your bed tonight, and since you're dragging me back tomorrow, I'm borrowing your clothes too."

"You're only in my bed if you're naked," I flirt and kiss her cheek.

"Won't be the first time." She smiles and lifts her shirt over her head, exposing her pale breasts.

Nope, definitely not the first; we've had plenty of fun together, and I love her for it. She's always had my back, and when I was feeling low and unattractive, she let me know just how beautiful she found me, turning me on to something I would never have guessed would be mind-blowing.

Don't get me wrong, we both love men, but occasionally it's fun to have a woman too.

VIKING

The next day...

SHEDDING MY SHIRT, I USE IT TO WIPE THE SWEAT FROM MY brow. The sleeves are ripped off, but it's no match for this Texas heat. Beads of perspiration run down my chest, and I quickly swipe over them too. South Carolina's hot, too, but it's a dfferent kind of heat, more humid than Texas. Here, I feel like my nuts are going to melt off.

"What the fuck could it be?" Nightmare hisses angrily, staring at his ride.

He has his bike partially taken apart; random pieces are strewn about in the motel's parking lot. I saw him get pissed and kick the old wooden picnic table outside, so figured he could use some help. We've been out here for a while and have gotten everything back together where it's supposed to be, but he's still irritated. I would be too if my shit weren't running right.

Letting out a deep breath, I pat the back of my neck with my shirt and then tuck a piece of the material into my jeans pocket, thinking about what the issue could be. "We've been over everything. The only issue I can think of at this point is if the gas had something in it. You filled up at that ghetto petrol station a ways out, and we all skipped it to eat. I'd clean out your tank with some fresh gas and hope that does it."

"If that weasel's selling fucked up gas and screwed my bike up, I'm going back and torching that fucking station."

Ruger steps out of his room, wiping down his piece with a cloth, right in the open. "'Sup." He chin lifts, and we return the gesture.

"Brother," Nightmare acknowledges.

"Talkin' about torching another place?" he asks, and I chuckle, remembering how much fun we had blowing up the last building.

Night shrugs. "If the fuck down the road sold me shoddy gas, I'm burning that shit hole to the ground."

"I'm down," Ruger replies.

"Yep, me too." I nod. If the owner has insurance on the place, we'd most likely be doing him a favor anyhow. It'd be good if Nightmare had a few of us watching his back as well.

"Has Scot mentioned a new job yet?" Ruger asks, and I turn toward Nightmare, curious as well.

I'm a bit surprised we've been stationary for this long considering we didn't get paid for helping out the Oath Keepers with their

California problem. I'm not hurting for money; I don't use much out on the road, but some of these guys blow through it like they have an endless supply.

"Nope, he hasn't said anything."

"Surely one of the Chapters needs more weapons; we haven't taken shit up to Montana in almost six months," he mumbles, but brings up a good point.

"He has a point." I cock my eyebrow at Nightmare, and he shrugs.

"I think Scot has a thing for the bartender," he confesses after we stare at him for a moment.

"You fuckin' with me? That bitch has been ran through so many times; she probably couldn't keep a dick in her twat if she tried to."

They both laugh as a car passes by on the old highway that runs between the motel and bar, gaining our attention.

"Goddamn!" Ruger gushes as the driver and passenger drive by slow enough for me to realize it's Cinderella.

Once it registers, I let loose a loud wolf whistle, trying to get them to stop.

Nightmare's lip raises a touch in his 'I don't ever fucking smile' sort of way, 'but this is the look you'll get when I'm amused.'

Ruger grins. "I could stick around for some chicks like that."

My temper ignites almost immediately, wanting me to teach his mouth how to stay shut when it comes to her, but I fight myself inside to hold back. Taking a few deep breaths, I begin to feel like my normal self again when a car turns into the gravel drive of the motel. It's not just any car, though; it's *her* car.

Ruger puts on a cheesy smile, strolling toward the passenger side that's closest to us. The girls have the windows rolled down and music blaring, but it gets quieter as they come to a stop directly in front of us.

Cinderella's gaze is trained on my naked torso while her friend is busy looking at Nightmare like she wants to eat him alive. I don't think she even really notices Ruger in front of her. She should, though, because Nightmare would easily break her.

Taking quick strides, I round the car to the driver side before Ruger notices that Cinderella's a twenty when her friend's barely a nine. He even thinks of touching her; I'll wire his mouth shut after I break it. Brother or not, I feel almost feral when it comes to her. I have no fucking clue why, but I'm damn sure going to find out.

She licks her lips, and my pants grow tighter at the sight of her tongue. She doesn't look like last night. She looks even better now—hair windblown, crystal blue eyes sparkling, wearing a little bikini top with short-shorts and flip-flops.

The savage inside me pounds his chest once I get a chance to take her in. I want to pull her out the car window, throw her over my shoulder and carry her straight to my room. I know that's not logical thinking, but fuck if I can't stop imagining it.

Her arms are scraped up a little on the backs; most likely from Shady fuck pushing her against the brick. She'll never have to deal with him again; I made sure of it.

I can hear her friend babbling on to Ruger about them being on their way to go swimming. I don't pay much attention, though, just gaze at Cinderella, cataloging each possible detail of her to memory. She's like an enigma that I can't figure out. What's so fucking special about her?

"Hi." She breaks the silence, and I'm forced to think of something to say. I have no idea what, so I just nod.

She chews on her bottom lip for a few seconds before swallowing and trying again. "So...umm, thanks for last night." She meets my stare, and I nod again like an idiot.

I hear Ruger ask if he can go swimming with them and her friend happily agreeing, inviting Nightmare along as well. Of course, Night doesn't say anything. He eventually looks over at the chick in the passenger seat, his nostrils flaring when she smiles at him.

She says please to him directly, and I think we're all surprised when he huffs, throws his wrench to the ground and strides to his hotel room, slamming the door in his wake. I don't know what the fuck that was about, but I'm leaving it alone.

Cinderella looks up at me again. "Would you like to come with us?"

Would I ever, but I won't. I know that if I see her in a bikini, I'm gonna fuck her whether she wants it or not, and I can't have her hating me before I even know why she calls to me so damn strongly.

"No."

She taps her fingers on her steering wheel, her gaze leaving mine to stare straight ahead like she's frustrated.

Ruger gets in the backseat, and I learn her friend's name is Bethany when she shouts it as soon as the back door closes.

"Let's go woman; I want a good tan before we go out tonight."

Cinderella shifts the car in drive. "Me too."

"Wait!" Spills from my mouth and her irises jump back over to me.

Her shoes.

I walk-jog to my room, grabbing the black heels off my table and bring them out to her.

"Oh my god, thank you!" She smiles, and my mouth goes dry. She takes the shoes, handing them over to Bethany, who's wearing a pleased grin.

Leaning over, I look through the window that's behind her seat, straight at Ruger. He glances at me, puzzled, and then rolls the window down. "'Sup?"

"Eyes off Cinderella," I quietly order, but it comes out more like an angry growl.

Ruger's eyebrows practically hit his hairline; he glances toward the driver's seat, and it hits him what I'm saying. "Got ya, brother."

Nodding, I walk behind the car back to my room. On my way, I hear her repeat 'Cinderella?' dreamily and Ruger says, "Yep, that'd be you darlin'."

I waited around for hours, checking out the window whenever I'd hear a vehicle and every damn time I'd huff when it wasn't them returning. Finally, I gave up, took a shower, put some clean clothes on and walked across the street to the bar.

Taking a seat next to Saint and Sinner, I'm pleased when a beer's set down in front of me almost immediately. I'm surprised they're here and not corrupting some woman with both of their cocks.

"Angel," I nod toward Sinner. He's not so bad, but he's always around to egg Saint on. He's the type to plant a seed in someone's head, then sit back and watch them self-destruct on their own. You won't catch him fighting much, but he sure loves to fuck with people's minds.

"Devil," I fist-bump Saint, and they both chuckle at me giving them shit.

They know those names are more fitting, though. Chicks eat up Saint's 'sweet boy' charade he plays to get in their pants. However, I see him away from the women. Trust me when I say the only type of angel he'd ever be is a fallen one, and nowhere close to a Saint.

I'm about half way through my beer when Ruger finally waltzes through the door. I wait with bated breath for Bethany and Cinderella to enter behind him, but they never do.

Ruger plops down in the seat across from me, looking tanner than he did earlier. He may have gone for Bethany, but I still want to pop his legs off and beat him with them for the simple fact that he got to hang out with Cinderella today and I didn't. I sat at the hotel pouting like a giant pansy ass.

"Where're the chicks?" I ask immediately. He better not have fucked it up with them.

Saint and Sinner's gazes both land on me as soon as the words leave my mouth.

"They went to go change; they'll be here."

"You found some new bitches for us, Ruger?" Saint pipes up.

"Naw, just me and Vike. They were in here last night playing pool."

Sinner's eyebrows shoot up as he does a low whistle. "Damn, it's like that, huh? I would've chatted them up last night to get some pussy, but I got the impression they were skittish."

"What happened at the lake?" I interrupt, my jealousy nagging at me, wanting to know every single detail.

"Not much. Cinderella painted her toenails when we first got there. Then she floated around the lake on a small air mattress and on the way back asked if your name was really Viking."

Saint leans forward. "No fucking way. Her name's Cinderella? The blonde one? I bet she's a goddamn fairy tale in bed," he finishes, eyeing Sinner.

Letting loose a deep growl, I slam my fist down on the table, hard enough to make the drinks bounce and everyone jump to catch them. I swear if he speaks about fucking her again I'm going to lose my shit. I'm not nearly buzzed enough to deal with bullshit comments about the woman I recently killed for.

"Damn, Vike, my bad." He holds his hands up in surrender. He's seen me get pissed, and no way in hell would Sinner be able to save his ass from my wrath.

Grunting in response, I turn back to Ruger. "You get some ass from her friend?"

I only ask because it was written all over her at the motel that she wanted Nightmare, not another brother.

"No, she's a fucking cock tease, bro. We hooked up a little, but she wouldn't let me get my dick wet, wouldn't even give me head. We had a few shots of tequila, but I'm hoping tonight she'll get blitzed and let me hit it."

Saint laughs and fist bumps Ruger, clearly approving of his less than stellar tactics to get laid. Can't say shit about it, though; we've all done it at some point.

Downing another beer, the night gets a little later before the girls finally show up. I'm fairly surprised to see her back so soon after the shit that went down. Most women would be locked inside their houses right now, too shaken up to leave. Is she just stubborn or could she feel safe coming back? Is it because she knows Ruger's here and that I will also be? Nightmare and Spidey-boy have joined us as well, leaving Exterminator to sit with Scot up at the bar flirting with the bartender he's got a hard-on for.

Cinderella walks her fine ass through the door wearing a fitted black leather miniskirt that barely comes to the bottom of her ass cheeks, paired with a red corset top and the shoes I gave her earlier. There aren't words strong enough to do her justice. Bitch makes my heart beat faster; that's the biggest compliment any woman could ever receive from me.

Surprisingly, Bethany holds her own. She fits perfectly alongside Cinderella, wearing daisy dukes, dusty cowboy boots, and a cut-up shirt coming to the bottom of her tits.

I swear to God, everyone at the table probably came in their pants a little at the sight of them. They're not just hotter than sin; they look like a biker's fucking wet dream, dressed like some badass bitches that belong on the back of our bikes.

"If you two don't want those chicks, I'll sacrifice myself to take one for the team," Spider offers and a few brothers chuckle.

Nightmare and I both mumble "shut-up," at the same time.

I catch it, but with the music on in the background, I don't think the brothers realize it was both of us who said it.

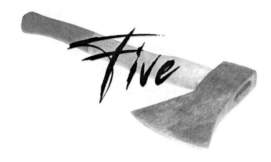

Five

VIKING

CINDERELLA CAME OVER TO SAY HELLO WHEN SHE FIRST GOT here, but I ignored her. Up close her tits were nicely displayed, taunting me with each breath she took as they moved slightly. I couldn't peel my eyes away from them. I'm sure if I had, my brothers would have been glued to her chest as well. My dick was so damn hard under the table; I couldn't think, let alone speak. She needs to cover the hell up if she's expecting some sort of a conversation to come out of me.

It's been sweet fucking torture to watch her each time, bending over the pool table to line up her shot. After each ball either one of them sinks in a pocket, the other takes a shot of liquor. I've been paying attention because I'm not letting them drive home if they're both plastered. Right now Cinderella's on her fourth and Bethany's on her sixth.

She glances at me briefly, walking around the pool table until she stops directly in front of our table. Spreading her feet apart, she bends over, her muscular legs on full display as she adjusts her pool stick until she has it where she wants it. She inhales a deep breath then pushes her ass out more while she takes her shot. With that motion, her skirt lifts the few inches I need it to so I can catch a glimpse of her bare pussy lips.

My fist hits the table top again, loudly, causing her to jump up. She spins around, her hand on her chest and eyes wide. My nostrils flare as I breathe heavily, wanting to rip the skirt completely off her.

"Are you okay?" She asks breathily and Saint groans beside me, no doubt witnessing what I was just privy too. I could go for punching him right about now.

"Pull your skirt down," I demand, glaring at her for making me lose control so easily.

"Fine," she huffs back. Wiggling slightly, she shimmies the tiny piece of material hugging her hips down. It moves all of an inch at the most, and I grit my teeth from her titties jiggling.

She faces Bethany, her long platinum hair falling to the top of her ass. "I need you and a smoke."

Bethany gets a wicked grin on her face and downs a shot before eagerly following Cinderella through the bar. Either she's happy about having a smoke or they're up to something. Whatever it is, those girls are fucking trouble. People think bikers are bad, but that bitch is the type to make a brother lose it over her, and that's gonna end up being me if I don't keep my distance.

Slamming the double shot of whiskey I had resting in front of me, I'm stuck listening to my brothers talk about how they all hope that the chicks have friends that look as good as they do.

"You going out there?" Nightmare asks quietly, so the others don't hear him over their conversation.

"Nope."

"Why the fuck not?"

Shrugging, I take a gulp of my beer.

"You know with the cunt shot she just sent you, she wants to fuck. If you don't jump on it, any other man in this shit hole would be happy to, Saint included." My eyes fly toward the other brother busy carrying on, drinking and having a good time, paying Nightmare and myself no attention. Nightmare raps his knuckles on the table. "Somehow I don't think you'd let anyone touch her, though."

"What do you know about it?"

He copies me, shrugging and sits back in his seat, taking a long pull from his bottle.

Goddamn it. Fine. I hate the fact that he's right. I would go fucking apeshit on someone if they touched her. She has me so wound up; I'm liable to flip out on anyone at this point.

"I'mma smoke," I declare suddenly, so everyone at the table hears me.

Night and Spider nod, while Saint, Sinner, and Ruger keep on reminiscing over our last trip to Florida. They turned into some regular beach boys, going surfing and shit. We gave them all types of hell for it, but they ended up loving it regardless of our opinions.

Trekking through the bar, I take a deep breath once I arrive at the door leading me outside where Cinderella is. I have no idea what the fuck to say to her or them both if they're standing there smoking and attempt to talk to me. I ought to make her put on my shirt while we're out back. It's the least she could do so I don't end up killing someone else for her tonight. At this rate, it'll end up being one of my fucking brothers.

I head outside, making sure the door closes behind me and that no one's followed me. I hope she was at least cautious enough to do that much as well. Standing beside it, I lean my tired body against the brick wall and dig a cigarette out of my front pocket, then my zippo.

It takes a few tries to get my smoke lit in the breeze, but it works eventually, allowing me a couple of drags before I hear the first soft moan. My eyes fly to the left of me where the building protrudes out in an 'L' shape.

In the full moon's bright glow mixed with the porch light, I can clearly make out Cinderella propped up against the building. They have the short leather skirt pushed up to her waist exposing her nakedness that I caught a glimpse of back at the pool table.

The real shocker is that Bethany's on her knees right in front of her, with her shorts pushed down to the ground. She has one hand between her legs, pumping away while her face is between Cinderella's thighs, licking furiously at her cunt.

Groaning, my hand immediately goes to my dick, squeezing it through my pants, attempting to ease some of the huge ache it's suddenly feeling from not getting the attention it wants. This is the last thing I was ever expecting when I got up from my seat. Cinderella's eyes meet mine as she moans again and I squeeze my cock harder. Fuck, I want in her so badly. This is no doubt the sexiest fucking thing I've ever seen.

Bethany starts sucking on Cinderella's pussy as her hand moves faster under her shorts; she squirms for a second before pushing her away. Bethany stays directly in front of her, using both of her hands to chase her orgasm.

Cinderella locks her gaze with mine again and inserts two of her fingers as deep as they'll go; my palm rubs my cock over my jeans, consumed by the sight in front of me.

Bethany calls out in bliss, finding her release as she watches Cinderella pleasure herself.

She pumps her fingers in and out, each time grinding her palm against her clit and moaning all while watching me. Cinderella's eyes suddenly fly closed, a loud moan escaping her as she rides the waves of her orgasm. The vulnerable look of surrender as she gives in and accepts the pleasure overcoming her body is fucking breathtaking.

She finishes and Bethany climbs to her feet, both of them wearing pleased smiles. Pulling my hand away from my dick, I take a drag off my forgotten cigarette as they fix their clothes, approaching me.

Bethany beams a bright smile as she passes by, heading back inside.

I'm panting like I just ran a fucking marathon when Cinderella gets to me. I'm expecting her to do the same as Bethany, but she pauses. Her blue irises take in my flushed face as her tongue glides over her lips, making my heart rate spike even higher from the simple gesture, and then she does something I'll never forget for the rest of my fucking life.

The bitch reaches her hand up, taking her two fingers she just came all over and brushed them against my mouth, leaving her wetness behind on my lips. It's more than I can handle; her scent on my mouth is my fucking undoing.

She flashes a sexy smile and disappears through the door. She's gone before I even realize it and I'm not sure if I'm in shock that she just did that or because she left me like this after such a brazen invitation. At least for her sake I hope that's what it was, or she's going to be highly pissed when I call her on it.

Licking my lips breaks me, and I go storming through the door, on a mission to have her. She thinks she can do that without any repercussions? I don't fucking think so. That bitch is so fucking mine; she doesn't know it yet, but she will real quick.

Once I make it through the hallway and into the bar, she's yet again bent over the pool table, just like she never left.

Perfect.

With a few powerful strides, I'm behind her; Bethany's eye's growing wide when she notices how furious I am. Cinderella gets a 'what' out to Bethany before I slam the top part of her body down onto the pool table. She attempts to move, but I hold her down with my hand in the middle of her back. She's no match for my strength no matter how hard she tries.

With my other hand, I release the button on my jeans, my zipper lowering immediately from my dick trying to burst out and lift her skirt up, uncovering half of her ass cheeks. She starts to scream in protest while everyone watches me claim her in front of the entire bar. After this, no one will ever touch her again around here.

"You offered your pussy up, Cinderella; now I'm fucking taking it," I declare and she quits jerking around as I slam my dick inside, seating it in her fully. Once she hears my voice, I can feel the muscles in her back relax some; the fight left in her is purely because I've decided to collect in front of everyone.

Gripping her hip tightly, I take her hard and rough, our skin making loud smacking sounds each time our bodies meet a certain way. Her pussy's tight, so fucking good, squeezing my cock like an angry fist.

Within a few pumps, I have her moaning, pushing her ass back into me for more. I give it to her, driving in deep until she whimpers, making my dick throb. The brothers all watch eagerly, no doubt enjoying the free show I'm giving them.

Nightmare's over at Cinderella's table. I'm guessing he was holding Bethany back from trying to stop me, but now she's sitting on his lap with a worried stare directed at her friend. His arms are wrapped around her front, holding her to him. She has no need to stress anyhow; I can feel her friend's cunt squeezing and pulsing inside, wanting to come.

"My bitch," I state loudly as I thrust into her, so everyone understands exactly what this means.

"Fuck you!" She yells, muffled from the pool table.

"I am, baby." Releasing her hip, I reach around giving her tittie a strong squeeze as I push my cock in as far as it'll go. She feels so fucking good; I have to hold my breath, so I don't go off to soon.

I hear, "Oh, Viking," followed by that same moan from outside; then her pussy is squeezing me over and over, soaking my cock with her juices as her body gives in to me. Grinding into her, she rides my dick until her orgasm finishes.

"That's it Cinderella, soak my cock; I want every last drop," I growl just before pumping her full of my cum.

After a few beats, I step back, moving my hand that was holding her down. She stays in place, though, so I go about pulling her skirt down first. Once she's covered up, I tuck my cock back in my pants.

Some of the patrons in the bar have stopped paying attention, while others are still staring. The music seems louder than before since the majority of the people are quiet now.

She takes a few breaths, carefully pushing herself up from the table. Once she has her footing again, she faces me, her blue gaze blazing with fury. I've never seen her pissed before; I think it makes her even more beautiful.

"My name's Princess, not Cinderella," she hisses angrily and follows it with a powerful slap. The crack from her palm connecting with my cheek is so loud that I wouldn't be surprised if it fucking echoed. The bitch hit me hard enough that my face feels like it's on fire, even with the protection from my beard. She's got some balls; that's for damn sure.

My hand shoots out, wrapping around her throat. Her eyes grow wide, and I pull her body flush with mine. I lower my face to hers, close enough that we trade breaths. "It fits," I mumble as she watches my mouth.

"Huh?" she whispers, meeting my eyes.

"Your name. You reminded me of a fairy tale, but Princess is better," I answer quietly.

Her hands flutter up to her throat, following my fingers down to my wrist and then further until she has a hold of my forearm. She clutches on, using it for balance as she gets to her tippy toes, making her a bit taller. It gives her just enough height to bring her mouth to mine.

She sucks my bottom lip between both of hers and immediately my grip on her neck relaxes, releasing her throat so I can kiss her. Her lips part eagerly when I take over, our tongues meeting and mating in their own form.

She jumps up, wrapping her legs around my waist, and our kiss changes from exploratory to downright erotic. Her body already wants more. I've heard stories from other brothers that once a cunt is claimed and filled with your cum that it goes crazy, wanting to fuck for days. They said it has something to do with breeding and finding your mate or some shit like that. I thought it was a myth, but maybe it's not after all.

My hands fly under her ass to hold her to me securely as I break our kiss, so I'm able to see as I walk. If this is happening, then I'm taking her to my room. I glance toward the brothers, getting a thumbs-up from Saint. I don't respond, just concentrate on walking toward the door.

Princess runs her tongue over my neck, sucking hard enough that tomorrow I'm most likely going to look like I was fucking attacked. I don't mind it one bit. I'll wear that shit proudly.

I can't believe that I claimed her in a bar, in front of everyone.

Where the fuck did that even come from? I'll think about it later. There's no way I can give a shit right now with her body pressed up against mine and her mouth on me.

PRINCESS

JUST KISSING HIM ALONE, IT'S LIKE DROWNING. NO MATTER how much I tell myself to struggle and fight against him, I succumb to the raging need he fills me up with inside. I want him, unlike anything I've ever experienced before.

There's never been a man in my life that was brave enough to fuck me like Viking did tonight. Any other women would be crying somewhere in a corner, acting as if they were violated from being manhandled, but I'm not most women. No, definitely not, 'cause I fucking loved it.

He was that hell-bent on showing everyone in the bar that he's the only one allowed to have me, well now I want more. That sample he gave me was only the beginning.

My tongue trails over the salty skin of his neck, nipping at the juncture meeting his shoulder. His cock is huge, pleasantly reminding me of its length and girth with each step he takes when it rubs against the bottom of my ass. "I want more," I declare, biting his shoulder between each word.

Groaning, he blows out a breath as his dick rubs against my ass again. We're nearly to his room already. He carries me as if I weigh nothing, taking large strides in a hurry.

His taste has left me in some sort of frenzy, wanting him any way I can have him. This isn't supposed to be part of the plan, sleeping with him multiple times. I feel lost, not wanting him to stop but at the same time my head chanting that it's not supposed to be like this. I never included in my mission the possibility of me actually wanting any of the bikers I planned on fucking.

We arrive at Viking's room, the key making a scratching sound as he attempts to stab it in the lock while juggling my wandering hands and me. He becomes impatient, slamming me up against the door. His closeness floods me in his scent of earth and leather. He's all man, everywhere, even his smell. Fuck, he makes my hormones race with all the possibilities.

Taking full advantage of his brief stillness, I hold onto his shoulders, pulling myself up a little way. He pauses, watching me lick my lips, and then I drop down slowly, grinding against his hardness trying to break free from his jeans.

Viking's cheeks flush, his eyes lighting with passion. "You don't hold the fuck still, I'm going to tie you up. Then I'll make you suck my cock while you beg for me to touch your pussy."

His words make me clench and ache with want. Luckily the door flies open as he finally gets it unlocked and we stumble through the opening. Viking starts to balance us, but I lose my grip, and we tumble to the carpet. He braces himself over me in the push-up position, so he doesn't land on me.

"Not what I imagined, but this position will work too," I chortle, and his lips part enough to give me a glimpse of his bright white teeth, clenched together.

Oh. He's not in the mood to play. I must have teased him a little too much.

"So, you like grinding huh?" he rasps with his face bent close enough I can feel the warmth from his breath flutter over my lips, taste the remaining whiskey left in his mouth from the pool table. He had thrown back a double shot right before he spurted his come deep inside my body, owning me in front of the entire bar.

I'd never been claimed before, and it's something I'll never be able to forget. The primal rage I felt radiating through his muscles as he powerfully drove into me over and over, then declaring I belonged to him in front of everyone. It wasn't only a declaration, but a dare. If anyone is remotely brave enough to approach me after tonight, then they become fair game for him. After what I witnessed him do to the last creep that threatened me, I know he wouldn't make false statements.

My heart doesn't stutter in fear thinking that there's a chance he could kill for me; no, it skips a beat, knowing for a fact that he really will kill for me.

His arms lower until he's resting on his elbows, his strong body blissfully pushed against my softer one. I've never felt small before with men, more on their level, but with him, he takes over every inch. Viking consumes me like no other, commanding me to submit and demanding control of everything. Shockingly, my body reacts as if it's being strummed like a melody, eager to please the one playing it.

Spreading my legs wide, my bare pussy lips become pressed against his jean clad cock, sending sweet torture through my body at the contact. "Yep," I eventually get out, starting to pant. He's so warm, his body heat blanketing me like a hot summer's day.

"Funny, when your tits are in my face, you always want to talk, but now that I have your pussy spread and wound up, you don't have much to say?" His hips press into me, delicious waves of pleasure slowly building me up higher

I manage a low moan, but nothing that makes any sense.

"My cock got you distracted, baby?" He pushes his jeans down enough, so his cock is freed, standing at attention, grazing the bottom of his belly button.

"My God you're big."

His mouth hikes up as he rotates his hips in a circle, his cock pressing into my clit perfectly.

"That's right, Princess, I'm gonna fuck your tight cunt until no other man ever measures up."

"Trust me; I can already confirm that they don't," I ramble, as his fingers reach between us, rubbing my entrance, collecting my wetness. Each time he touches me or grinds into me, I feel my juices flooding, dribbling down toward my ass.

"You save your voice 'cause you're gonna be using it a lot tonight. I'm going to fuck you so hard that tomorrow your legs will shake when you try to stand. Each time you sit, you'll burn, but be reminded that I was there all night long. I'm going to have this pussy as much as I want, then I'll take your mouth." His hand moves lower, stopping at the entrance of my ass, the one place that hasn't ever been touched by anyone. "And when you think you can't possibly come again, I'm going to make you cry, baby." He shoves two fingers deep into my back entrance, a gasp escaping me at the new sensations, and he continues, "Yeah, you're gonna cry and beg me to stop, but I'm gonna fuck your ass, and after you're cleaned up and done crying, I'm going to spray my thick cum all over those pretty titties you like to flaunt in front of me. You may hate me by morning, but you'll fucking be mine." He ends on a growl, plunging his cock into my core while continuing to play with my ass.

He's right, I scream.

I scream in absolute fucking wonder at the amazing feeling of being taken by a real man. I should've saved my voice because it was only the beginning.

Six

PRINCESS

I'M AWOKEN BY A REVVING CAR OR TRUCK ENGINE COMING from outside. My body aches in new places, spots that I've never felt sore before, reminding me of last night. Viking had taken my body like a man possessed, never getting his fill, and I'm definitely feeling it all over. The sheets smell like us, leather and flowers. I would never have guessed that it would be a good mix.

The mattress beside me moves, and I crack my eyes open to witness his firm, naked ass as he stands, pulling on nothing but the jeans he was wearing the night before. I love the Nordic tattoos he has scattered over his arms, including one the size of my entire hand on his thigh. His entire back is covered in one massive tattoo as well. The details are breathtaking, making the Oath Keepers patch appear more sinister and threatening. The flag being held by the skeleton looks like it's being ripped from his flesh to wave proudly. It must have taken hours and several sessions to get something that would probably win an award if it were ever put on display. That would never happen; my father wouldn't approve of such exposure to his club or the surrounding Charters.

My father.

I wonder if what happened last night in the bar has gotten back to him yet. Surely someone must have said something about the dramatic public claiming performed by a notorious Nomad. Hell, it should be the talk of the town and surrounding area with how much people like to gossip.

Fuck my life. I can't believe I let that happen.

I'm probably going to end up having to move away when this is all said and done. I won't put my mother through added stress; I do, however, have to complete my mission. The things Viking did to me, made me feel…I'm such a fool to believe I could get through this without any damage to myself.

He would never truly make me an Ol' Lady, and God knows I couldn't handle everything that comes with that title in the first place. I'm too much like my mother, an old soul. I want monogamy; I want a husband who comes home to me after work, and I get to cook him dinner every night. I couldn't deal with having a man that came home when he wished, fucked whomever he wanted and ended up in prison.

I'm not that strong, neither was my mother and she's taught me plenty. Last night should be enough, and I can keep my distance from Viking in the future. Between him and the Prospect, I don't think I could do anything else with another member. I know I said before that I would be with a dozen if that's what it took, but something's changed.

Viking's different for me; he's a game changer. I don't feel disappointed when I look at him, but the opposite and that scares the fuck out of me. I can't afford to let myself fall for a biker. I won't let him break me like my father broke my mother.

The motel door closes quietly on Viking's way out. I guess he knows who that engine belongs too.

Their voices are loud enough to carry through the poorly built motel and over the rumbling from the exhaust. It's hard to tell if it's a friendly visit with the heavy metal music playing amongst everything else. Despite my stomach telling me to stay in bed, that Viking can handle whatever's outside, my feet hit the matted carpet.

I scoop up the thin sheet, wrapping it around me and make a beeline for the door.

Opening it enough to fit my body through, I lean against the doorjamb, curiosity spurring me on to be brave or stupid. Immediately I notice two of my father's men, each standing next to a mean looking black beast of a car. The doors are wide open with the windows down, allowing the thumping from the rock music to escape into the parking lot.

Breezing over their cuts, I learn that the driver is my dad's Enforcer, Cain, and the passenger with the bright Mohawk is the club's Treasurer, Spin. They notice me immediately. Mohawk guy's face lighting up as he runs his eyes over my sheet. The other guy stares, his forehead wrinkling slightly like he's trying to place me from somewhere. He won't be able to, though, my father's never introduced me to these guys before.

The driver keeps talking through his curious gaze. "So 'bout that barbecue, my Ol' Lady's cooking and she doesn't mess around when it comes to food."

Viking and a few of his brothers stand next to the bike Nightmare was working on yesterday afternoon, listening to my father's men.

"Aye then, laddie, we're always up for some good cooking." A robust, red-haired man beside Viking answers in a Scottish accent. I've never seen him before, but he wears the same cut that Viking has, so he must be one of his Nomad brothers as well.

The Enforcer grins, a set of dimples coming out to play that make my stomach flutter a little. Fuck, he's hot. He doesn't have the same effect on me as Viking but damn is he nice to look at.

"Bring your Ol' Ladies too. I know the girls would wanna meet them." His friendly gaze meets mine causing Viking to glance between the other men and me.

The Treasurer stares openly at me as well, clearly enjoying what he sees and then like an afternoon storm coming out of nowhere, Viking's irises blaze.

Facing me, his nostrils flare as he breathes deeply, taking in my bedroom attire. He looks upon me with such heat; I can't stop myself from licking my lips nervously, remembering his taste. He had that same intense fire blazing last night while he took me relentlessly. He'd kissed me until I swore my face would be rubbed raw from his beard.

My fingertips lightly trace over my chin, finding a tender spot at the memory.

Spreading his legs out a little more, he crosses his arms over his chest, his shoulders becoming even wider by the new stance. His magnificent body's completely imposing, overtaking more space than what should be allowed; it seems like he grows even larger as he commands everyone's attention and points toward his room. With a deep grumble, coming out more like a growl he demands, "Get in the room."

Huffing in irritation, my temper flares to life, ready to spit nails if necessary. I open my mouth to protest, and he dutifully cuts me off.

"Now, Cinderella."

Glancing over to the men, I wait for someone to tell him he's ridiculous, but I notice they're all staring at me, not him. They've got on amused smiles and smirks, entertained at this biker bossing me around. My gaze settles on Viking again.

His eyebrow lifts, almost in challenge. It's like he's warning me that he'll put me in my place if I argue. This man clearly hasn't seen every side of me; I don't do well with taking orders. Well, orders that aren't sexual anyhow.

He'll learn—the hard way.

Keeping my mouth shut, I spin around and give them my back as my temper takes over. Being one that doesn't easily relent, I slam the door behind me. Making sure the impact is strong enough that it echoes through the nearly empty room, sounding like a clap of thunder, making the fake art on the walls shake.

The guys outside chuckle loudly at my outburst and the thin walls of the motel allow the sounds to float inside, taunting me, angering me further. Gritting through my sore muscles and my ass that feels like it could be on fire today, I slide on my leather skirt.

Glancing around for my corset, I land on a new package of wife beater tank tops. Those will be much more comfortable than attempting to squish my tits back into my top from last night.

I hated wearing it. Damn thing squished me like crazy, but it was all about the look. Ruger had told me that Viking would for sure be at the bar last night, and I wanted any advantage I could think of to get his attention. I would never have returned to that place had I not known Viking was there along with Bethany, just in case I needed help again. I hate to ever feel dependent on someone like that, but I learned my lesson the first time, going outside alone, barely two nights ago. My arms and back still have the stupid scrapes to remind me of my bad judgment call.

Throwing a tank on, I practically drown in it, so I tie it up at my mid-back, leaving a sliver of skin on my belly visible. I'm probably looking like a hot mess, but I couldn't care less. I'm making a point to this bossy biker, that he doesn't give me orders outside the bedroom.

Shit fuck. I like him being such a demanding ass. It's sexy to meet someone who's so damn Alpha; at times I worry my panties will catch fire being around him. Oh wait, I'm not wearing panties. Regardless, he doesn't need to speak to me like that in front of so many men.

Viking had been sweet enough to retrieve my purse from my trunk last night about halfway through our activities, so I snatch that up. Quickly, I shove my corset top inside the oversized bag that should most likely be classified as luggage rather than a purse. Tossing my shoes in also, which Viking admitted he's a bit obsessed with, I shoulder the wide strap and head back outside, ready to leave.

Bethany's standing next to Nightmare, this time, clad in his T-shirt and boxers with hair shooting every which way like she just climbed out of bed as well. I wonder if she got to hook up with him after all. When we went home to change she confessed that she was interested in him.

What's it with these grouchy fucking bikers that pull you to them? Nightmare seems broody and miserable, but she's still fascinated with him. Who am I to talk though? Viking could be classified as a quiet asshole, yet he has me twisted all over the place for him.

Nose and chin up, I use a dose of fake confidence strutting past the men and call back, "Come on, Bethany, we're out of here." Since I'm not in my high shoes and the gravel doesn't bother my bare feet too badly, I put a little extra swing in my hips making a few of the guys' mouths pop open.

Viking lets loose a frustrated growl, and it takes everything in me not to shoot him a smug smile in defiance. "Where do you think you're going?" he demands, but I ignore him.

"I'm coming! Let me grab my stuff," Bethany answers and runs back into Nightmare's room.

"*Princess*!" he shouts. His voice is strong and lethal with a warning ingrained in my name, just by his tone.

Turning to him and propping my hand on my hip, I give him 'the look,' "What?"

"Where do you think you're going?"

"I'm leaving."

"I'm not done with you."

Shrugging, I don't get a chance to respond as Bethany comes running out, yelling that she's ready.

"Fine. I'll call you." He plays it off.

"Sure you will," I retort, knowing damn well that he doesn't have my number. He didn't get it last night and I damn sure didn't leave it for him.

Bethany and I trek toward the two-lane highway, the guys loud enough I can still easily overhear their conversation.

"Her name's Princess? Or you call her that?" Cain questions Viking.

"It's her fucking name. I call her Cinderella. What's it to you?"

I try to do a sly glance back, but catch Cain openly staring at me, as if he saw a ghost. I don't think twice about it, though; there's no way he knows who I am.

"Definitely, bring your Ol' Ladies with you to the barbecue," I catch him saying right before we're too far away to hear anything else.

VIKING

CAIN REPEATS HIMSELF, AND I ALMOST POP OFF THAT SHE ISN'T my Ol' Lady, but I did claim her last night. Whatever the fuck that means now, I have no idea. I was planning on hashing it all out with her later today, but that plan's gone to shit with her temper tantrum.

It's none of his business right now anyhow. I can't stand Ares, but the rest of the Charter here doesn't bother me much. Cain, for example, is good people.

At the same time, I don't want to say she's not my Ol' Lady 'cause if another brother goes after her, I'm liable to scalp them. The bitch was already under my skin, but after last night—getting a real taste—it's even worse. She makes me feel as if I've had my first hit of heroin and I want more.

Fuck! She came outside in a goddamn sheet, and she wants to give me attitude for it? I know these brothers and what goes through their heads. The moment they saw her dressed like that, there's no doubt that they were picturing the fucking fabric falling.

That's my fucking property; I own that body and the only time I want her seen in so little is right beside me. At this rate, she'll end up on the back of my bike permanently, and I'm not so sure that descript-ion fits with being a Nomad.

The chicks speed off, Bethany waving and smiling as they pass by. Princess stares straight ahead like we're not over here, still pissy I reckon. Good thing I remembered to use her phone to send myself a text message with her number once she had passed out. I doubt she'd have given it to me today.

"All right bro, we're smashing. Don't forget—three p.m. next Saturday." Cain fist bumps each of us, Spin doing the same before climbing back into the midnight black Hellcat. I'm not much for cars, but that's one badass vehicle.

The car creeps through the parking lot, and we all admire the impressive machine, throwing up a few fingers in a friendly wave.

Spin leans forward, cranking the music up as the car hits the highway and Cain romps on the gas. The powerful horsepower of the Hellcat sends Spin flying back into his seat, and we all chuckle. You know Cain did that shit on purpose since the brother touched his radio. I'd probably do the same.

"Fuck, I wanna drive that car!" Ruger wistfully declares, watching it speed away.

Saint claps him on the back, nodding, "Bet it's one hell of a pussy magnet." He turns toward Sinner. "We need one, man. Both of us in it, I bet bitches would be throwing themselves on the hood."

Sinner chuckles, shaking his head.

Nightmare snorts and rolls his eyes. "Whatever, I'm going back to bed."

The brothers agree and head back to their rooms. I won't sleep, though. I hardly got any rest last night, and I can't stop wondering what Princess is up to today.

Sitting on the picnic table, I light a cigarette and pull out my phone, turning on the screen. She's my new background, sleeping peacefully —fully naked—and absolutely fucking beautiful.

Spider takes a seat next to me, getting a peek at my device.

"Hmm?" Grumbling, I flash an annoyed glance his way for not minding his own business.

"She sure stormed off quickly."

"No shit."

"Do you wanna talk about it?"

"Of course not, why would I?"

"Look, man, you're the one clearly pissed about it and thinking of her; I'm just lending an ear if you need it. What's so fascinating about this one anyhow?"

"Fuck," escapes with a sigh. This guy likes to chatter all of a sudden. He's been so quiet up until recently, and we've gotten along just fine. "Hell if I know."

"You're too picky."

"Excuse me?" My eyebrows wrinkle as I take a pull off my smoke.

"We all see you sift through which bitches you allow to suck your cock and the few you fuck. This latest one, you took her in a bar and then all night, I'd guess by the whimpers and moans I heard through the wall. You can't shake her because you don't just fuck anyone. I wouldn't even call that just fuckin' either. I heard you being all sweet and shit when she got upset. You care about her, enough to console her."

"You've all seen me fuck in public," I defend.

"Yep, we've seen you fuck on the side of a building and in a field at a party, but brother you claimed her in front of a room full of people. You mounted her in front of the brothers and everyone else in the middle of a bar, just so another man wouldn't touch her." He breathes deeply and mutters, "You're royally fucked, bro."

Shrugging, I glance up, watching the clouds filter over the sun. "Doesn't matter. She was pissed and left. I'll probably never see her again." Leaning back on the table with my elbows, they prop me up enough so I can stretch my legs out in front of me.

"Do you wanna?"

His question catches me off guard. Do I want to?

Squeezing my eyes closed tightly, I admit the truth, muttering, "Fuckin' A."

"Let me see your phone."

My eyes fly back open as I face him. "Why?"

I don't want him staring at Princess' picture; it's all mine.

"Because I'd bet five hundred bucks she gave you her number or you took it."

"You're not calling her." I take one last puff and throw the rest in the rusted coffee tin. *I need to quit that shit; the road hides most of the smell, but I still know it's there.*

He grins, his face appearing younger with the lightness. "No, but do you want to know how to find her?"

"You can do that?" I reply, sitting back up, my interest suddenly peaked.

"Seriously, think about who you're talking to right now." He places his palm in front of me, waiting for me to hand over the phone.

"Let me change something."

"I already saw the picture; I won't yank my dick to it, I swear."

I shoot him a brief glare, then give in, nodding and hand over my phone. My eyes never leave the device as he illuminates the screen. He quickly flips to the apps section and pulls up some tech shit about the phone. Spider loses me from that point on. I have no idea how he can know so much shit about technology, but if it finds her, I'll be grateful.

He chants, "Come on, come on, come on," quietly to himself, tapping his thumb against his jeans as he waits for something to happen on the screen. After a beat, he lets out a cocky chuckle full of triumph.

"How do you find her?" I'm assuming it must've worked by the grin he's back to wearing.

"I installed a program that works like Key Logger."

My expression mirrors my thoughts, becoming more puzzled.

He tilts his head and tries to explain again. "It's like the Key Logger program you install to monitor someone's computer activity."

I remain quiet, not having a clue what the fuck he's talking about. We didn't have money like that, for useless shit such as computers when I was growing up. It was hard enough to eat when I was fucking hungry.

Huffing, he simplifies, "It's an app that's going to track where she goes."

"She'll blow the fuck up knowing I'm tracking her."

"It's a ghost program; she won't be able to tell you're tracking her. Even a decent phone tech wouldn't know about it. You'd have to be a programmer or app builder to know where to begin looking."

Cocking my eyebrow in disbelief, he rolls his eyes.

"Look, man, I give you my word. Princess won't find this shit. Besides, your phone is an unlocked burner; she'd have no idea who it belonged to unless she knows your number. Does she?"

"No. I haven't contacted her."

"Yet." He mumbles, causing me to scowl. "Okay, it's finished." He holds the phone so I can see everything also. "Click apps. The box with a crown as the photo is her, click it."

Multiple options appear such as find, log, points of interest, home, listen, disable, and the last—delete program.

He hands me my phone. "The question mark next to each word will tell you what the option does, otherwise, just click on the words, follow the prompts, and it'll take you where you want."

Nodding, I mutter, "Appreciate it," while my eyes stay trained on the words, curious what they'll each do.

"I'm your brother, Vike. I'll always have your back."

My gaze meets Spider's as he stands and I fist-bump him, giving him the respect he deserves. It's easy to forget that these men are my allies, and they support me. I was surrounded by snakes for so long, that it's been hard to let go of the shit I dealt with in the past. Never again—these men are different, respectful, and loyal.

We tap knuckles, and he heads toward the office while I pull the app up again.

I start off by clicking the question mark next to the word 'find.' It's labeled in red, so I guess that one's the most important. A small white cloud pops up with a paragraph inside explaining that you use that option to find the person that's connected to the tracker.

Let's see if this shit works or not.

Holding my breath, I press the red lettered option. Google Maps opens up and hones in on a street view, showing me the last recorded image of the area. Below the picture, an address appears in white.

Let's see just how accurate this thing is.

Nodding to myself, I stride over to my bike and dig out my Bluetooth piece from my saddlebag so I can hear the directions my phone gives me. Once it's securely in my ear and I've clicked 'go' on the phone, I toss the cell into my saddlebag.

Mounting my ride, I quickly tie a bandana around my head and place my half shell helmet on securely. With a loud rumbling engine, I steer my way through the gravel lot, hitting the highway, a man on a mission.

Seven

PRINCESS

I DROPPED BETHANY OFF AND THEN CAME STRAIGHT HOME to jump in the shower. I'm still sore from Viking, and I'm in serious need of a nap. That man has the stamina and strength of three men put together. When he got going, it was impossible to think about anything but him.

Once I'm not a zombie, I'm soaking in an Epsom salt bath and drinking water. I'm sure I need to rehydrate. Digging through my dresser, I find one of the large men's white T-shirts that I prefer to wear to sleep in when I'm here alone.

Pulling it over my head as I shuffle toward my bed in a sleepy haze, I hit the cool sheets, sliding between them and my big fluffy white feather down. My comforter's like a giant pillow, and it's pure heaven to sleep under. I close my eyes and my stupid cell rings.

Are you kidding me right now? Don't answer it.

It finishes its three-ring cycle then almost immediately picks up ringing again.

"Oh for fuck's sake." Complaining, I sit up, the covers falling to my waist as I reach for the irritating device.

Bethany glows on the screen. She'll just keep calling back, so I swipe my finger across the screen to answer.

"Hmmm," I mumble into the phone and crawl back under the

covers, making myself comfortable.

"You're sleeping right now?"

"Ummhmm."

A loud cackle comes through the speaker causing my eyes to fly open in irritation. "What?"

"I just find it amusing that you finally met someone who can outpace you."

"Shut up."

She laughs loudly again. "Oh hell no. You drug me back there last night on a mission, which means I'm owed details and have the right to give you shit if I want to."

"You looked pretty cozy this morning coming out of Nightmare's room. I doubt it was a hardship for you."

"You're not turning this around on my night. You were irritated in the car, so I left it alone. I didn't pressure you, knowing Viking's dick was probably in your mouth most of last night, and I didn't want to experience that on your breath. You've had time to shower and mouthwash, so spill it."

"I can't believe you just said that."

"It's the truth, though, isn't it?"

"Why are you so nosey?"

"Yep, I knew it. You weren't angry at him bossing you this morning; you were heated because you liked it. In fact, I'm betting the entire time you spent in the shower; you remembered all the things he did to you."

"I can't talk about this right now. You know why I had to be with him. It's done. Now I need to find another."

"Another? Honey, are you crazy?" I know by her tone that her eyebrows are raised so high, they're probably closer to her hairline than her eyes.

"I may as well be. I can't believe I thought Viking was going to be an easy target."

"Look, I tried to warn you, but you saw it as a challenge instead, and now you're deep. What you pulled last night with me outside, basically egging him on to watch us and then giving him your orgasm? You opened him up to a whole new playing field. I don't know what you said or did to that man when I went inside, but even I know that after a biker claims you the way he did in that bar, you won't be having another."

"I hardly doubt he was sincere. You saw his brothers; there were no women with them that were more than a one-night stand."

"Hey! How do you know I was just a one-night stand?" she responds with a bit of hurt coming through her voice.

Hmm, I wonder what that's all about, why she'd be upset. Bethany's never minded before, always stating that she knows what it's all about and wants to have a good time.

"I knew it; you did fuck him!"

"We'll talk about me another time; right now, it's about you and Viking."

"There is no me and Viking to discuss. Did I sleep with him last night? Yes. Do I want to again? Yes. Am I going to? No way."

"You have it so bad."

"I'm taking my nap now."

"Princess, you need to call your mom." She sighs and my heart pings at the thought of my mom. I miss her.

"Why, so Prez can answer? No thanks. I'll call tomorrow morning when he hopefully won't be around, and if he's still there, then at least I know he'll be sleeping until noon like he used too."

"Okay, just...just don't push her away. Some of us aren't lucky enough to have a mother in our lives that love us so much."

"I know. I'm sorry if you think I'm a spoiled bitch about this whole thing; I've just seen her so hurt each time he leaves. She shouldn't have to cry for days—sometimes weeks—barely eating and moping around because some piece of shit doesn't realize how wonderful she is."

"You know I don't feel like that. I understand why you're this way. If I had someone like your mom in my life, I'd do everything I could to protect her and get her some payback for her pain. I'm on your side, and I'll always be, even if I don't think you're doing the right thing."

"I know. I love you," I respond, and my body relaxes with her reassurance.

"I love you too," she replies, and I hit the end button, turning my screen off.

Setting the phone next to my head, I roll over on my side, tuck my hands between my thighs and close my eyes. If it's cold enough, then this is my favorite way to sleep. I can still smell him, the leather and spice that seems ingrained into his skin. It smells amazing. And mint, from his mouthwash, it was all deliciously overwhelming to my senses.

I must doze off for a few minutes because I swear I can hear myself snoring, but that's not what startles me, it's the pounding on my front door. Someone's knocking so loudly, you'd swear the place was on fire or something.

Keeping my eyes closed, I pull the covers off my face and sniff the air a few times. *No fire.* Taking a few deep inhales, I attempt to get my mind back to nothing when the door lashing begins again.

Jumping up in a furious rush, I storm toward the front door. "Whoever the fuck this is, better be dying if they're hitting my door like that!" I huff to myself and the random houseplant placed next to my couch. I'm not a morning person, in general, and this lack of sleep is liable to make me scratch someone's eyes out.

Wrenching the door open in a flourish, I shout in a tired fit of rage, "What?"

On the other side, my eyes meet with a muscular chest covered in black leather.

My gaze flutters over the different patches decorating the front, one, in particular, drawing a swift gasp as I read over each letter. -**Viking-**

Fuck, shit fuck, fuckity, fuck! How many times has Brently warned me to check the peephole before opening the door? I've no doubt learned my lesson; you better believe I'll be using it from now on. How did he find me? What's he even doing here?

He stands so stagnant; he could be a statue. Clenching my fists, I meet Viking's intense stare.

I expect to find heat or the cocky confidence from last night, but instead, it's turmoil swirling in the colorful depths. He's confused like he's questioning something, maybe wondering if he should've come here.

Lacing my voice with venom, I ask the million-dollar question, "What're you doing here?"

His nostrils flare like an irate bull, ready to charge. "You left," he rasps, making it sound more like an accusation rather than a declaration.

"We fucked, it was obviously done." Shrugging my shoulders slightly, I continue, ready to drive it home and piss him off enough to leave. Anger and words have always been my defense I go to when someone can hurt me. "Besides, I always want a shower right away after a one-night stand. Don't you?"

A deep rumble shakes his chest as anger consumes his handsome face; suddenly his hands fly forward, each one grabbing my upper arms tightly enough to leave finger marks. Viking prowls forward, lifting me off the floor, and driving me backward into my living room. He kicks out behind him, effectively slamming my front door so hard there's a good possibility it could be broken.

A whimper bubbles up, leaving me, shocked at the sudden movement and the ferocity overcoming Viking's entire being. I've never been manhandled before; no one that I know would've dared to touch me like this. There wasn't a man that I dated brave enough to stand up to me or fight with me. If they had, my brother would've beaten him to a pulp if I hadn't already.

My back meets the wall next to the hall leading to my bedroom, and my head hits the solid surface with a small thump, momentarily dazing me. My stomach twists with a rush of adrenaline as the flight or fight reflex starts to kick in, commanding my body to survive. I want to struggle against his hold, to fight him, but my heart pleads for me to just stop this nonsense and apologize to him.

He releases one of my arms, bringing his hand between my legs. On reflex, I slam them closed around his palm.

"Open your legs, Princess," he demands sternly.

"Fuck. You."

"God, you're one mouthy bitch; of course, you'd be the one I'd find."

It takes everything inside to hold back from dropping my father's name. I refuse to let him win this battle for me. I can stand up for myself. I have to.

Viking releases my other arm to peel my thighs apart. I'm in pretty decent shape, but in no way am I strong enough to fight off the mountain of a man in front of me. Slapping my hands over his pecs, I drive my fingernails in as harshly as possible.

I'll make him feel something.

I'm expecting him to cry out in pain or surprise—anything. His gaze, simmering with rage, meets mine, and he smiles. The motherfucker grins like it feels good, exactly the opposite of what I wanted.

Two of his thick fingers drive inside me, stretching my tender flesh, going as far as my body will allow them. Every piece of me is wracked in confusion. I gave myself freely to him last night. Why is he here, why's he doing this?

A cry escapes me at the intrusion, while my pussy excitedly milks his fingers. The trader bitch has already been broken by him and is ready to do what he commands.

"Why?" I whisper brokenly, as a tear falls, cascading over my cheek until it drops from my jaw.

He stares into my eyes intently; breathing deeply as if he's just running a race and pumps his fingers into me a few times. "Because I made you mine," he murmurs.

Another tear drops as I attempt to speak, "I-I…"

"Who's in bed with you Princess?" His question catches me completely off guard, as if him finger fucking my pussy wasn't enough of a distraction that I can't come up with a response quick enough. "I *said,* who's been in *my* cunt today?"

Clearing my throat, my eyes hold steady with his. "What are you talking about Viking? No one's here, I came home alone."

"You're naked under this shirt; your hair's a fuckin' mess, and your face had the just fucked look on it when you answered the door. Your friend here eating pussy again?"

Swallowing, my tears slow as I'm starting to understand why he just flipped out. A little, but now I can see how he would come to this conclusion.

"No, I haven't been with anyone, just you last night."

"I'll be able to tell," he retorts, his gaze dropping to my pebbled nipples.

"What? How?"

Viking slips his fingers free, showing them to me, covered in my wetness. "Like this." He sticks the fingers in his mouth, sucking the juices off them completely. As he tastes each digit, his cock grows rock hard between us, digging into my belly.

The site of him so turned on from a small taste is insanely hot. My breaths quicken as his cheeks flush, tattling that he wants me very badly. After his fingers are clean, he drops his hands, lightly grasping my hips and I relax my cat claws that've probably drawn blood under his shirt.

"You swear she wasn't licking on you?" he asks—his voice softer, normal—vulnerable. "I'm able to tell by your flavor; no man's had you but me. I can't tell, however, if she had her tongue on you."

I damn near stutter, rushing to respond. "I promise, no one, not even Bethany. I was asleep when you knocked; that's why I looked like that, and I always wear this to bed."

A deep breath leaves him as his shoulders finally relax. I can smell myself on him, and it's making me want to jump him.

"No one fingers, licks, or fucks this cunt but me now. You're *my* bitch."

"Umm, no. I'm not anyone's bitch."

His eyebrow rises, staying perked up for a few moments as he holds me hostage, waiting for his argument.

"I claimed you last night in front of everyone. Like it or not, you're my Ol' Lady now. You belong to me." He takes a step back as I desperately attempt to fabricate a response to justify why I'm not his Ol' Lady, nor could I ever be. Opening my mouth, he interrupts, "I'll give you space, but get your ass to the bar Thursday night. I'm going to have a few drinks, and then I'm eating that pussy for dessert."

And I'm speechless.

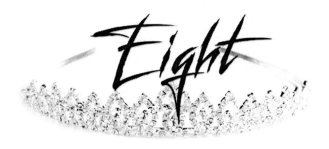

Eight

PRINCESS

"WAIT A MINUTE…YOU'RE TELLING ME HE DID ALL OF that and then just left you there? He didn't make you come first, say I'm sorry or anything?" Bethany's mouth hangs open in shock.

We're sitting on a small patio having lunch at a deli we like to eat at. I was filling her in on the whole Viking situation from yesterday when he overtook my apartment and then left me hanging.

Shaking my head, I take a sip of my bottled water.

"It happened exactly like I told you."

"Jesus Christ," she replies and takes a bite of her sandwich.

"I know. I pretty much froze up like an idiot."

"I still can't get over the fact he got you to shut up." She snorts and I shoot her a glare. "What! It's the truth, Prissy, and you know it. You have to be the most argumentative, loud-mouthed person I know. And I say that in a good way, take it as a compliment. You stand up for yourself and your beliefs."

Rolling my eyes, I dip my sandwich in my loaded potato soup and take a huge bite.

"Good thing you have a big mouth; I bet Viking's dick is huge."

My hand flies up to cover my lips as I damn near choke at her words. She says some random crazy shit. Chewing my mouthful carefully, my eyes water as I swallow the food down and clear my throat.

"I almost just died right then. Don't talk about his cock anymore."

"You're very much alive honey, and if you choke like that with his dick in your mouth, there's no doubt he'll shoot off like the Fourth of July."

"Shush, tell me how it went with Nightmare."

Her smile drops, and she briefly glances away. "Another time, we need to go, or we'll be late for our movie."

What the fuck happened and why isn't she dying to talk to me about it?

"You win this time, but you're telling me eventually."

She nods quietly and collects her trash, then escapes anymore conversation by going and throwing everything away.

I swear he better not have hurt her already.

VIKING

Three days later...

THURSDAY ROLLS AROUND BEFORE I KNOW IT AND FUCK IF I don't want to admit it, but I'm looking forward to seeing Princess. If I'm real about it, I've been thinking about her non-stop since I left her place. It's taken everything in me these past four days to leave her alone and not show up unannounced again.

I haven't completely left her alone, though. This app that Spider hooked me up with is like my secret weapon. Tracking her has been a fucking dream come true. Every place she drives to and stops, it logs on my phone with the complete addresses. Then there's the listening feature; I've been able to turn it on at random times and catch her voice. She can't hear me, which is perfect.

Fuck, I can't wait to listen to her moan when I'm inside her later.

With four days apart now, I assumed my attraction for her would dim and I'd be able to cut her off, now having had a taste. I'm a fucking fool. Staying away has driven me mad. I'm irritated about everything, grouchier than usual, and when I manage to fall asleep, I dream of her every damn time. Probably doesn't help that my bed smells like her flowery scent.

It's constant, utter fucking torture knowing what she looks like sleeping next to me and wishing she were in my bed, or how silky her skin feels when it's up against mine, and how hot her tight cunt feels squeezing the cum right out of me. That bitch fucking owns me. I know it already, and soon my brothers will also. If anything, that's pissing me off even more.

Being a Nomad is my life. I love being an outlaw and doing whatever the fuck I want, never being judged for scalping a motherfucker who crosses me. Right now Princess stares at me like I'm a god or some shit, but I know eventually that light will fade away, and she'll look at me with blackness, finally seeing the type of poison I really am.

When I was growing up, I dealt with that look from my mother, but my father couldn't give two fucks. He's even darker than I am. But Princess is my exception. I would hang myself or slit my goddamn throat if I ever saw the poison shadowing in her gaze.

With those thoughts, I angrily storm across the street to the bar. I'm early; I know she won't be here for a while, but I need whiskey and a lot of it. It won't solve my issues, but it'll help drown out any guilty feelings I'm having. I've turned off my conscience; I've had to, in order to become the ruthless bastard that I am today.

Princess, though, she lights a fucking fire inside my chest and with the many chances of me damaging her eventually, I need to start drowning it out now. When it comes down to it, I know that no matter how much I tell myself that I'm no good for her, I don't fucking care. I want her, and I'll have her.

"Whiskey. Double. Neat," I demand as my ass hits the stool and Stacy's eyes grow wide.

"No problem, would you like a beer too?"

"No. Keep them coming or give me the fucking bottle."

She nods, rushing to pour me half a small glass. Placing it dutifully in front of me, she stares up at me a little frightened. I almost feel like I should pat her on her head and tell her good job, so she doesn't piss her pants. I don't, however; instead, I grunt and swallow back the entire beverage, placing the glass down louder than necessary.

"Another one?" she asks before reaching for the tumbler.

"Did I stutter?"

"Okay then. You've had a shit day, and I know you're not driving, so how about I just keep pouring them until you've had enough?"

"Good girl." I nod, and she pours a hefty amount of the spicy, amber liquid.

Saint plops down next to me, sending Stacy a dazzling smile. Her face brightens at his light ash colored irises and good ol' boy charade he has her fooled with.

"Rough day brother?" He questions, gesturing to my liquor as Stacy places his Captain and Coke down. "Thanks, sweetheart." Saint winks and she flutters away in a daze.

"It is what it is, man."

"That's the fucking truth." He sighs and takes a hefty gulp.

"You got Sinner hiding in your ass somewhere or what?"

"Fuck you. He'll be over later." He chuckles and shakes his head. "You're not ready to hit the road yet? Usually, you're restless by now."

Shrugging, I finish my drink, catching part of two guys' conversation. Saint starts to talk again, but I'm trying to concentrate on what the other guy's saying. Holding up a finger between us, Saint notices and instantly quiets to pay attention also.

After a few beats, I'm able to locate the source. It's the stupid Prospect I ran into when I first saw Princess. Their voices grow louder as he gets wound up, making it easier for me to overhear everything.

"She was the sweetest I've ever tasted man, swear to fuckin' God! Blonde everywhere too; fuck, it was good."

"Damn, blonde pussy hair too?"

"Yep. When she told me her name was Princess I thought the bitch was joking, but I could see it with her looks an' all. Then she told me her father's the President of the fucking Oath Keepers! Was the dumb bimbo tryin' to get me smoked? Her old man would fall the fuck out if he found out."

"Scratch, you're good as dead even if Prez doesn't find out and one of the brothers hear about it. You know they'd string you up, messing with a family member like that."

"That's what I said too. I got the fuck outta there like my ass was on fire and shit. Don't get me wrong; I'm not saying I'd never hit it again. I'd probably have her come over for a midnight booty call then send her packin' out the back door, but that's about it, so my ass doesn't get shot."

This motherfucker needs to shut up. I've pretty much heard all that I can handle. It's a miracle I haven't broken something already, but I was concentrating on what was being said.

Saint's ashy irises—now dark and stormy—meet mine, having heard it all for himself. "That your little Miss Happily Ever After they're talking about over there?" He nods toward my next kill.

A furious growl resonates through my chest, unable to answer him as my fury builds inside like a Phoenix, destined to rise from the smoke and seek out retribution.

A malicious grin appears on his too pretty face as the real Saint decides to show himself. "Oh, let's have some fun, shall we?" He lets loose a loud chuckle, getting to his feet. "Been far too long since Sinner's let me play with someone, always keeping the peace." His eyes widen in glee. "What do you wanna do to him, Vike?"

"Get him out back; the bathroom will be too messy. It's about time I pay a visit to the club and let them know where the fuck I stand." He nods turning away.

Saint cackles as he saunters toward the two Prospects, excited to finally stir up some trouble. Snatching up his drink, I finish it in two swigs, watching as he claps the loud mouth Prospect on the back, filling him full of lies about wanting his opinion on a bike outside that he may buy.

Scratch, being green, follows Saint willingly out the back door as the other Prospect sits at their table, happily chugging a cheap draft beer. I wish I could come up with some sort of plan, but I'm honestly raging so much inside that the image of ripping him apart, piece by bloody piece runs through my mind like my own personal horror movie.

Standing, I move throughout the bar in a daze, not focusing on anything but the bristling need to get outside before I burst. If I'm confined for much longer, I'm liable to kill someone in here or at least break a bunch of shit that would end up getting the cops called on me. Laughter and voices are nothing but a blur, everything mixing as I make it to the back door.

Slamming through it, the Prospect's head whips toward me at the loud noise, fear and trepidation quickly consuming his features as he discovers it's me. He shuffles a step back behind Saint, gullible and stupid to think that my brother would ever save him. He's a nobody, and Saint owes him no loyalty.

Saint turns to Scratch wearing one hell of a scary looking smile and grabs his arms forcefully.

"Hey, what the hell?" Scratch yelps in surprise.

Striding toward them, I grumble, "Most of you candy-ass motherfuckers like to run when I approach them."

"What's this about? I'm cool, remember?" he pacifies, causing Saint to laugh.

Saint loves when they beg and plead. He'll torture a fucker for days just to see how long they'd cry for their life. That's where Sinner comes in, cleaning up the mess and putting the miserable to rest. He's always alongside Saint, ready to help keep a sense of balance.

"I heard you talking about my Ol' Lady."

"No way; I was talkin' about a chick I met at a party. I wouldn't be talking about your Ol' Lady."

At my glower, Saint snickers, squeezing the Prospect's arms until he yelps and faces him.

"Fuck! What's your problem now?" he asks angrily.

Saint smiles brightly, confusing Scratch, then drives his forehead into the man's nose when he's least expecting it. Blood showers them both as Scratch cries out in pain, feeding into exactly what Saint wants.

"You don't speak unless spoken too, Prospect," Saint orders and I take a few steps closer, ready to take what's owed, unsnapping my large blade as I approach.

"No one speaks about Princess like that. You think her cunt tastes good? It'll be the last one you ever taste, so savor that shit. I won't walk around knowing some motherfucker has touched my bitch and fuckin' lived," I growl, leaning down close to his face, showing him who the real alpha is.

Sweat draws on his brow as he swallows, thinking of something to placate me, "Sh-she wasn't yours. I wouldn't do that."

"No," I respond quietly with a brief chuckle, "that's where you're wrong, Prospect. She's always been mine." I finish and watch the shock hit his face as I drive my hunting blade deep into his kidney. The fucker was too stupid to pay attention and try to get away. Not that he could've, but it would've been more entertaining for us anyhow.

Saint tosses the wounded man onto the ground, watching as he falls on his back, crying out in discomfort. Once he starts apologizing and trying to bargain with us, Saint lowers to his knees above Scratches head.

Giving him the nod, I unstrap my hatchet and sheath my blade. Saint's hands fly to Scratch's skull, securing it so he can't squirm away and cause me to miss. Planting my heavy, size fourteen boot on Scratch's chest, I brace him to the ground with my weight.

"Ready?" I ask Saint, and he cackles maniacally, excited at what's about to happen. We've gotten into some shit together a few times and each one he's been the same way. Torture and killing bring me satisfaction if anything, but it fills my brother with energy and happiness. I can only imagine what kind of life he had to shape him as he is. Mine was fucked up, but I have a feeling his was like nothing I'd ever imagine.

"Do it, Vike!"

Bending my left knee as much as I can behind me, I position myself as low as possible in the perfect spot over the Prospect and grip my ax with both hands. It's much harder than one would expect, driving the blade through flesh and tendons, and fuck, there's so much blood. Not to mention my height making it harder to decapitate someone when they're flat on the ground as well.

Glancing at the man's terrified eyes one last time as they fill with tears, I say my piece, "I've already killed for her once motherfucker; you're just another one under my belt. I'll be goddamned if anyone disrespects my woman like that and lives. I may not have been her first, but best fucking believe, I'll be her last."

At that, I swing the ax aiming directly for his throat. The first hit makes a decent implant, but not completely sufficient. It's with the second swing that his blood splatters enough to hit my boot resting on his chest.

Saint laughs with each chop, getting covered in blood and loving every minute of it. Eventually, I have to get on my knees to get close enough so I can finish sawing through the last remaining fleshy pieces. The small stuff is always the hardest to get severed.

"Saint, you need to get cleaned up, you're a mess. Call Spidey to help you dump the body."

His gaze meets mine, his brow furrowed. "Why aren't you dumping it?"

"I need to pay someone a visit."

"Okay then," he answers, pulling his phone from his pocket as I grab the short hair on the Prospect's skull. He has just enough for me to grip it; hopefully, I don't drop it.

Saint climbs to his feet, swiping his tongue against a few drops of blood on his wrist and follows me around the side of the bar. He watches as I mount my bike, still holding the bloody head in one hand. I've ridden having to hold onto shit before, so it's not that difficult being that I'm a seasoned rider.

The engine comes to life, loudly announcing our presence and within seconds, I head toward the Oath Keepers MC Compound. I have something that belongs to them, and it's time they know that I'm not fucking around.

Neither the kill nor the quick ride to the clubhouse does anything to cool down my temper. Normally a long ride will do me wonders, giving me enough time to clear my head out and come down from when I rage. If I were smart, I'd hit the road straightaway after my pit stop, but I know I won't. I've had one thing on my mind nonstop, and I plan to have her as soon as possible.

The Prospect that's posted at the gate sits up suddenly when I come into sights. He takes one look at my extended arm, still tightly gripping onto the head and stays clear, so I can ride through without any issues. Smart move on his part. I wouldn't kill him if he tried to stop me, but he'd damn sure learn.

Having worked with this club in the past, I know the kid's calling up the Prez or VP right now to announce my arrival. It's exactly what I want him to do, get either of them to come outside. I plan to throw this motherfucker's head at the pussy-ass VP's feet then let the Prez know his daughter belongs to me. I did this club a favor, taking out their biggest threat not even weeks ago, and it's time they show me that they're grateful.

Easing off the gas, I slow down some more, eventually rolling to a stop not far from the main entrance. The Compound consists of a fairly large building that houses members, their chapel, kitchen, and a bar. Off to the side is their shop where they fix bikes and the occasional vehicle. The land it all sits on is surrounded by a tall electric fence and who knows what else.

It takes merely moments before the lot of them shuffle out. Ares, their VP, comes to a stop directly in my path as several of his brothers flank his sides. Cain, his Enforcer, takes the right, then Spin, the treasurer, and finally, their newly patched member, Shooter. To his left stands 2 Piece, the Road Captain and gun trader, then Twist, the unholy one covered in tattoos. He's the fucking crazy brother I've heard of. I thought he was going to join the Nomads for a while, but he backed out eventually. Lastly, the President's son himself, Snake.

I could probably kill half these motherfuckers before they got me down. Scot says we're friendly with them, and Cain's not bad in my book, so I offer a warning instead of bullets. I may be an Oath Keeper, but when it boils down to it, this Charter is not mine. I would support them when needed, but I ride with the Nomads. We make our own fucking laws.

Staring coldly at the VP in front of me, I release his Prospect's head—the heavy skull more resembling a bowling ball than the lump of mush it is at this point. As it rolls across the asphalt, heated by the scorching Texas sun, it eventually stops, sticking to a particular hot spot on the pavement.

He doesn't flinch, so my gaze expands, taking in the other members beside him. "Tell your club to stay the fuck away from my bitch. I won't say it twice."

Ares' eyebrows shoot up, his nostrils flailing as he breathes heavy, attempting to reign in his temper. I've heard about him too. He used to be the Enforcer for the club, known as the Butcher for sawing bodies up.

That's cute. I like to hack my kill up too. Only I drive my hatchet into their body repeatedly or sometimes scalp them, using my favorite blade to pull their skin away, exposing the angry red flesh underneath. I'll happily teach him how to be a real fucking butcher if he'd like.

"The fuck you do to my Prospect?" he eventually grumbles, angrily peering at the decapitated head.

"He thought he could touch my Ol' Lady then talk about it. I didn't agree."

Cain's hand flies to his forehead, massaging his temples as he mumbles a disgruntled, "Fuck."

Ares glances over at him, "Brother?"

Cain drops his arm flashing a look at Ares, then meets my stare. "The blonde from the motel when we were there? Princess?"

Snake's head snaps over to me at Princess' name, and I nod.

"You sick fuck!" Snake shouts, charging at me only to be held back by a few of the men.

Ignoring him, I speak loudly. "You've all been warned what will happen if you touch her. Don't even fucking look at her." Pointing at the head stuck to the pavement to drive my point across. "Now…get me the Prez."

Ares chuckles, shaking his head. "You're a ballsy fucker; I'll give you that. What do you expect's gonna happen when you tell the Prez you've claimed his little girl as your Ol' Lady and you never even asked him?"

"I don't give two shits what's going to happen or if he'd have given me his permission. There's nothing to discuss; she's a grown-ass woman. I fucked her in front of an entire bar full of people and let every goddamn one of them know that I own her. Just like I don't give a fuck what any of you think about it."

Snake makes a sound reminding me of a roar as the guys hold him back from charging at me again. The dramatics are interrupted when the heavy metal door leading into the clubhouse slams closed, announcing the Prez' presence.

Snake shoots his mouth off before the older man even makes it off the four steps leading to the parking lot. "He has Princess! This dick thinks he can claim her. Tell them to let me go so I can slit his throat."

Prez sighs deeply, striding toward us with purpose. "Brently, stick a sock in it, son. You have any idea who you're threatening right now? You're a Prospect, son of mine or not; you shouldn't be speaking right now."

Snake breaks the guys' hold, storming off toward the shop. Probably angry his father just called him out in front of the other members.

Prez comes to a halt next to Ares. He claps him on the shoulder affectionately. "Thanks for handling this son, but let me have a talk with him."

Ares' brow furrows, his irises growing lighter as he relaxes and allows the Prez to take over. I can see why he was the Enforcer for so long; he's definitely the protector who loves his club. I can't stand him, but I do respect that bit of him. "You need me, I'm here," he mumbles, taking a few steps away and lighting a smoke.

Watching him, Prez huffs, "Your Ol' Lady's gonna have your ass if she catches you out here smoking again. You want babies and don't I remember that you agreed to stop if she'd get knocked up?" He glances at the others standing around. “Someone give him some gum before Avery chews him a new one on his health and he takes it out on the brothers.”

Rolling his eyes, Ares stomps on the cigarette, then folds his arms over his chest. If the situation weren't so serious, I’d laugh. I guess his Ol’ Lady’s a stubborn one like my Cinderella.

The older man’s kind gaze meets mine again. “Last I checked, your cut said Oath Keeper on it. You’re welcome here, so how about you get off that bike and take a walk with me?”

“I’m not the strolling type, how about you just get out what you have to say.”

“What did he do?” Prez gestures to the Prospect’s head, so I fill him in on everything, including the part where his daughter’s now my Ol’ Lady. It takes a while to explain everything and eventually, I’m off my bike, walking with him along the fence line as I talk.

Shocked is probably the most accurate word to describe him at my news. At first, he didn’t believe me, but when I described her looks, her car, where she lived, etc., he started to realize I was telling the truth.

“Out of everyone, she ends up with a biker and a Nomad at that.” He shakes his head in disbelief.

His boots suddenly become interesting as he stares down at them and thinks it all over, the Prospect no longer on his mind now that his daughter’s involved. I don’t know if the man’s happy or about to come unglued. One thing I’ve noticed is that he’s hard to read about how he feels about anything. He could probably win a grip of money if he ever decided to try his hand at playing poker.

“I would never have pictured her with someone like you,” he finally continues. “Prissy tell you that she was a good girl growing up? Went to college, stayed out of trouble. She hates me with a passion, but that’s all right; it kept her safe overall.”

“We haven’t talked about her past; it’s all happened pretty quick.”

His eyes find mine again as he smiles slightly. “It always does. It was that way for her momma, and I fuckin’ fell hard for her, and best believe she had a temper like no other.” The happiness falls from his face, his gaze growing firm. "Just don't fuck it up. Her and I, we've grown so distant, I no longer have the privilege to make demands with her anymore. I lost the right to tell her who to love and be with when she gave up on me being her father. In many ways, I'd love to put a bullet through your skull, but in the end, I have to be grateful that she ended up with a member and a strong one at that."

We walk back to the parking lot, continuing our discussion.

"She knows I'm a hard man." It's the best answer I can give. I know I'll screw up sometimes, what matters is if I can fix it.

"I fucked it up with her mother—worst mistake of my life. When I tried to go back and fix it all, club threats against Princess and Brently started pouring in from my rivals. I had to let them go. It was the hardest thing I've done, leaving my family and letting them hate me. Tell me, you have kids, can you walk away from them and your Ol' Lady, then not look back to keep them safe?"

Adjusting on my bike, I sit back a little and reply truthfully, "No."

"So you're the selfish type."

"Hell, yes, I'm selfish. She belongs to me—they would belong to me. Best believe I would hunt down every last motherfucker with the balls to threaten my family. I'd feed them their fucking nuts as my entertainment and then take their lives as my payment."

"I thought I could too, tried for years, out on the road looking for any of them." He sighs. "It drove my children away from me, caused my Ol' Lady years of heartache. At some point, you have to figure out your limit. You ever reach that, you come find me so I can help you sort things."

No matter how sad his sob story sounds, I can't find it in myself to feel any type of sympathy for him. I grew up with a fucked-up family. I know firsthand what that's like, and I'd never put someone through that experience.

"That's the difference between you and me, Prez. Princess is my limit. She's the type of woman I'd happily kill a hundred men for. I'm not saying it'll be an easy life for her; in fact, she'll fucking hate me at times, but I'll do my best every day of my life not to break her. And I'll damn sure protect her."

"Good. I still receive threats against my family, had one awhile back from the Twisted Snakes. Fucked my boy up pretty good and threatened my daughter next. We snuffed the fuckers out, but the danger's always out there. The main thing is that she never knew about any of it."

"I'll keep her out of my business, but I won't lie to her."

"She knows you were comin' here?"

"Yeah, she helped me chop his head off," I retort, deadpan.

Chuckling, he approaches me. "Let's keep this between us then."

He reaches his hand out, and I shake it in return. I'm not making any promises, but it won't be a conversation I bring up to her first thing.

"You won't have issues from any of my brothers or my son for that matter. I hope you're able to bring her around with you; I'd love to finally see my daughter. This club's her family, too, whenever she's ready for it."

"I'll see you around, Prez." Replying, I crank the engine over, the loud rumble overshadowing anything else he'd been planning to say.

He throws up a two finger salute as I walk the bike backward a few paces, his men all standing around Ares, no doubt waiting to be filled in after I'm gone. Had this whole situation not been about his daughter, though, I can't help but think that I'd have a bullet through my skull right now for chopping off his Prospect's.

Nine

PRINCESS

STARING AT THE BEAT-UP BUILDING, I LET LOOSE A LONG sigh. After questioning myself fifty hundred times today about whether or not I should show up to meet Viking, I decided to say fuck it and drove my ass to the bar. Debate about it all I want to, if I'm not here, then I know he'll be knocking on my door again. I can either face him in a room full of people when he's had a drink or when we're alone, and he's irritated again.

Bethany's supposed to meet me up here once she's showered and changed from work. I still haven't gotten her to confess what's up with Nightmare. I'm quite stunned at her persistence; any other time I've been able to crack her into confessing. Her silence is making a huge statement, and I'm hoping that with her showing up tonight I'm not setting her up for failure being around Nightmare. It's been four days since she stayed with him, maybe they've had time to cool off.

Crossing the threshold of the noisy bar, the music, and rowdy patrons' conversations envelop me as I start to scan the room for Viking. Halfway through my perusal, one of his brothers approaches me. He's a lot smaller than Vike, but still pleasant to look at with his dark features.

Stopping right in my path, he shadows me by a few inches. I'd guess him at five foot eleven or so. His sharp jaw is overtaken by at least two days of dark stubble from forgetting to shave, or not caring enough to.

A friendly smirk plays on his lips until my gaze meets his amused charcoal colored irises. "'Sup Princess." He flashes me a bright smile that's slightly bashful. "Sinner," he states, his hand grabbing mine lightly to lead me farther into the bar.

Confused as to why he's touching me, I follow a few steps before he continues, "My brother had a few things to take care of, but he'll be back in a bit."

Requesting any details, even something simple like what time he'll come back, would be a waste of time, so I keep quiet. I know how bikers and their business work, thanks to my mom's constant rambling about my father and his MC rules. It's been drilled in that you keep your nose out of their club stuff, not only for your safety but also because it'll cause pointless arguments.

The bartender notices Sinner approach and rushes over, ignoring the other customers waiting for their drinks.

"Refill?" the older lady questions and he shakes his head.

"Nah. Vike's Ol' Lady needs one of those red girly things you make." Her mouth turns up in a friendly coffee-stained smile, and then she's off busily mixing liquor and juices for me.

I wish I got service like that when me and Bethany order. Instead, it's usually a dose of attitude and a shitty made drink.

Cutting straight to the chase, I lift my palm up, covered securely with his. "Umm, why are you still touching me?"

"Just being friendly to my brother's Ol' Lady."

"Thanks, but please stop calling me that and I'm able to walk myself." Using my other hand, I point at my shoes. Dutifully he looks down. "See, I have two feet just like you do."

He flashes me a hurt glance about to say something, but the bartender approaches stealing his attention. Once he's thanked her and has my fruity drink in hand, he starts to tug me along toward the back tables.

"Where are we going?"

"You can come sit with the brothers while you wait. No one will bother you back here."

"Oh. They won't mind?" I'll admit it's nice of him to offer. Getting attacked by the creep was traumatic enough that sitting at the bar alone is slightly intimidating even if I am inside and surrounded by people.

"Nah, they're cool."

"And Viking?" I only ask because I've seen how he acts when another male's within two feet of me.

"Trust me; he'll appreciate you being at our table when he gets here." He plays it off as a random idea, but I figure it's so he can keep an eye on me for his brother; either way, though it's a win-win for me. I get to relax with a few free drinks and at the same time know I won't be harassed again.

Two sex and the beaches later, along with an abundance of information on the guy's latest conquests, and I can understand why Viking rides with them. Sure they're scary looking and at times crude, but overall there's a strong bond forged. Their easygoing nature and friendship with each other are enough to make any outsider want to be included.

With the vodka and sweet juice mixture working its magic over my self-preservation, I interrupt their banter by blurting out the thought that's been running through my head all day. "I need to break it off with Viking. It was only supposed to be a one-night stand, yet I've seen him a few times in the past couple of weeks and then there's tonight."

Collectively, the entire table of men quiet. Each one is staring me down, looking as if I have the plague, and they don't know what to do with me exactly.

"I tried to after what happened the other night, but then he showed up where I live, and I'm sure you know he's persuasive when he wants to be."

Spider cracks a smile, thawing the frigid awkwardness I'm suddenly surrounded with.

Taking a large gulp, I stammer on, "The man's beyond bossy. He's temperamental and demanding and....and each time I stand up to him,

I swear he grows an extra five feet tall." Flailing my hand dramatically, a few of the guys' expressions lighten, amused at my description of their brother.

Scot, the older red-haired biker laughs to himself and Spider speaks up. "So, you're saying that you stand up to him?" His irises sparkle as he glances briefly at his brothers like he's conveying a silent message that I'm not privy to.

"Of course, I do. Don't you?"

The table erupts in loud chuckles and Spider nods, laughing with them. "No wonder he can't leave you alone."

"Aye, 'tis a good thing," Scot agrees, winking like he's proud of me.

They move on, picking their previous conversations back up without skipping a beat, and I grow quiet with my thoughts. Staring out the dingy pane of glass in the window beside me, my original plan that Bethany came up with plays through my mind again. Only now I feel incredibly guilty when I think of it instead of excited. Not guilt for my father, but for planning on using Viking. I should be happy right now, being one step closer to making my father miserable, but I know to do that, I'd have to give up Viking.

What do I want more? Viking? Or revenge?

It's been no time at all; how can this even be an issue already? Sure, I've seen him a few times over the past few weeks, but think of those times. One was me escaping and being too chickenshit to speak to him. The second time, I was taunting him and got freaking attacked, which he saved me from, thank God. The third time, I teased him to no end with Bethany, turning him into some kind of amazing sex god who fucked me in front of a room full of people. The last time I saw him, he mauled me, thinking I was sleeping with someone, and then stormed off.

Yep, that's the extent of our relationship. It's been the most thrilling, life-changing experience of my life so far. What in the hell is he going to do to me if we stay together for six months? I'd be completely ruined for anyone else. Like he wanted to happen when we slept together, it'd happen with my heart as well. My vagina's already given up; she was waving the white flag the first time she saw him.

My heartbeat starts pounding stronger in my chest as I watch Viking pull into the gravel parking lot, rolling to a stop under the bright street lamp.

Minutes pass with him remaining on his bike, not moving to dismount. I can't make myself turn away nor do I want to, as I watch him eagerly. His ominous figure practically glows from the lamp overhead and the pitch blackness fanning out behind him, makes him appear incredibly powerful. Something must be on his mind to just sit there, lonely, not hurrying in for a drink. He knows I'm here.

I can't wait any longer. I talk a good front in my mind and to him, but every time I see him, my insides melt. He's like gravity, keeping me to him, even if I try to jump.

Leaving my seat without another thought, I weave around people trying to play pool and dance. My legs dutifully carry me through the bar and outside until I'm left standing in front of Viking, feeling more feminine than ever next to the powerful rumble of the huge machine between his legs and his needy gaze.

My mouth parts, drawing in a swift breath as I'm close enough now to notice the blood splatter that's covering his jeans and arms. Suddenly my mind's plagued with memories of the first time I met him. The image of Viking gripping the man by the throat, and then staring at my exposed chest is almost too much to think of. He may have saved me, but I could read it in his intense glare that he wanted to take me just as badly as my captor had.

"Get on." He breaks the silence, and I swallow.

"I don't ride."

Viking's nostrils flare as he revs the engine louder. "Didn't ask. Now climb on."

The liquor in my system does the trick, providing me with enough courage to place my palm on his solid bicep. Holding on securely, I swing my leg over the back. I've seen my dad and brother mount their bikes countless times, so I have a general idea. There's not much of a seat for me, just a small piece of padding wrapped tightly in black leather.

His other hand reaches back, landing on my exposed thigh, warming it instantly with his touch. Gripping my leg firmly, he slides my body forward until my breasts are molded against his back, and then he wraps my arms securely around his muscular torso.

Viking's so solid; holding him to my body like this makes me feel the safest I've ever been. I know I'm with a man who's able and willing to protect me; he's in control, and he's already made me his. He's also everything that I've never wanted but is turning out to be everything that I've always needed. I can feel myself healing. In just a short time, he's helping my anger fade away, replacing it with his heat.

Viking's movements are so quick and efficient it takes me by surprise, and the next thing I know, we're entering the highway with me holding on for dear life.

Too scared to look around at first, I take in the broad stretch of the endless dark sky above us. The stars twinkle proudly as he takes his time, steadily increasing our speed and making the ride pleasant. I've never ridden a bike before and with Viking being a seasoned rider; I'm guessing he can tell. Most people would never believe me if I was to admit I'd never been on a bike before, being the daughter of an MC President.

After about ten minutes of the quiet highway, my muscles and grip on him start to relax as I grow more comfortable being behind him. Laying my temple against him, I close my eyes and just breathe, taking in the peacefulness of the whole experience. Once we started going faster, the stuffy Texas air swiftly morphed into what I'd imagine a thousand butterflies kissing my skin would be like.

Time passes all too soon it seems, and I feel him start to slow down. Parting my lids, my senses become overwhelmed. The leather on his cut hits my nostrils, along with an undertone of exhaust, the humming vibrations growing stronger each time he downshifts sending delicious pulses to my core.

My pussy grows wetter with each passing mile, a sinful torment as I do my best not to squirm and chase my pleasure. The last thing I want is to cause a wreck when he's showing me this other side to him. He'd probably never forgive me for ruining his motorcycle and this beautiful night. Judging by the blood decorating his clothes, it wasn't so pleasant for someone else.

At a bump in the road, Viking's bike shifts, the movement causing a powerful enough tremor to hit my clit. He must hear my whimper escape because he slows down, pulling off at the first abandoned dirt road he finds.

The bike comes to a complete stop and my heart pounds so erratically he has to be able to feel it against his back. My breath comes in silent pants; I'm so damn turned on after the sweet torture my pussy was just put through.

"Get off," He barks, causing me to jump.

"Ex-excuse me?"

"You heard me; get off the fucking bike, Cinderella."

At his words, I suddenly feel like there's a frog in my throat. I don't know whether to laugh at his nerve for ditching me way the fuck out here or cry. I'll most likely scream and throw what I can at him but then I'll get so angry that I'll end up crying. Who can blame me, though, we're out in bum fuck Egypt, surrounded by fields. It'd be pitch black if it weren't for the million stars and nearly full moon. With my luck, I'll be hoofing it home and get so nervous; I'll have a full-on anxiety attack and pass out on the side of the road.

Carefully I dismount, watching, so I don't graze any of the pipes or engine with my legs. That would be a miserable reminder of tonight. I learned about them getting hot when Brently was a kid and burnt his hand on my dad's pipes. That ER visit took forever as my mom kept having to explain that she didn't burn or abuse her kids.

Standing beside his massive thigh, I prop my hands on my hips and hit him with a glare that's so cold you'd think he'd turn to ice. "You have a lot of nerve."

"That so?" His gaze flicks to mine, eventually dropping to run over my body.

"Hell yes. I can't believe you're actually kicking me off your bike here," I retort angrily, gesturing to the emptiness around us.

"Well, maybe you shouldn't have been rubbing your tits all over my goddamn back. Your nipples are so fucking hard; I can feel them through my fucking cut!" he shouts back fiercely.

"My nipples? You have got to be joking right now. If you weren't too busy driving like some kind of maniac maybe, the wind would be warmer!"

"So it's my fault?"

"Of course. You're the one who brought me out here. I told you back there that I. Don't. Ride."

Viking peers down at me with his mouth drawn in a stern line, making me feel like I've been naughty and now I'm in trouble and about to be punished. It almost makes me want to lash out at him some more to see what happens.

Those thoughts flourish as his massive hand shoots out, snatching my bicep with rough precision. He yanks me toward him like I'm some rag doll, weighing nothing at all. Unable to catch myself quickly, my stomach collides with his thigh. The impact is forceful enough that it damn near steals the breath from my lungs.

I should be furious with him for manhandling me each time a situation escalates, but being so close to him has pure carnal desire running rampant through my veins. Beating my fists on his solid pecs, I halfheartedly shove against Viking and prepare to let loose an outraged scream. Pretending to fight and struggle like this, will only spur him on further until he satiates the ache building between my thighs the bike ride initiated.

On our first night, he had to hold me still as he took my virgin ass. I'll never forget how thick Viking's cock grew when I'd whimpered and attempted to move away. He'd stopped at first to try and ease the ache by coating the rim, inside and around my tiny puckered entrance. It felt sinful and erotic having him use the warm cum he'd filled my pussy with moments prior.

I'd begged, offering my mouth and pussy again while he'd worked his way in slowly. Then my tears came, and he fucked my virgin hole like a man obsessed. Fuck, it hurt but eventually his skilled fingers played with my clit until he had me calling out in ecstasy.

My cheeks blush, thinking about that once-untouched area, now fully being his. Someday he may want it again. I know it'll hurt for a while until I'm used to it, but I don't care, it's worth it.

As if Viking can read my thoughts, his mouth slams down on mine, ravishing my lips like he's famished and can't get enough. His dark scruffy jaw prickles my sensitive skin and turns me on more, knowing he's one hundred percent man. I love it when he's this way. There's nothing soft when he gets like this. His muscles are like rocks, his kisses relentless, his movements harsh, and his cock stiff.

One hand tangles in my long hair, gripping it tightly against my skull as his tongue takes mine hostage, demanding it to surrender to him.

Meeting his hunger, my tongue twists with his, hoping to entice him even further. My body's brimming with so much need that if he brushes against my pussy, I'm going to come.

He frees my arm to grab the front of my shirt roughly where they cover my breasts, twisting the material tighter against my skin. Viking's mouth overtakes my every thought as he kisses me crazily, sucking my bottom lip between his and then pulling away to nip at my top one playfully. Not ready for the erotic moment to end, I draw his tongue into my mouth, sucking and rimming it like I would his cock, greedily taking whatever I can.

Within seconds, he's breaking off our lip-lock, panting and flushed. The crimson coloring his cheeks, more pronounced from the pale moon, reveals that he wants it just as badly as I do.

My mouth's left tingling in his absence, the rough whiskers bestowing a bittersweet memory as the night air tickles my skin. His soft lips leave mine behind, swollen and eager for more. I refuse to beg no matter how badly my body wants me to.

Viking's dark gaze drops to my chest, enraptured as my breasts rise and fall from my excitement. "You're not wearing a bra," he murmurs absently, and I shake my head out of habit, not needing to respond.

The evidence is clear with my peaks stiffly pleading for his attention. He loves my breasts; I left my bra at home purposefully for him.

He clears his throat, his voice gruffer than normal as he demands, "I've got what you need, climb on." He leans back some more, sliding closer to where I was sitting on the way here.

Viking turns my body and then lifts until I climb back on the bike. This time, I'm facing the handlebars like I'm the one driving us. Staring out at the openness in front of me, I begin to panic. "I can't drive." Plus, his bike's massive, literally the biggest I think I've ever seen.

A deep chuckle comes from behind me as I feel his large, warm palm rest between my shoulder blades. "Baby, you'll never drive my bike. You belong on the back. And before you lash out with some smartass retort, I mean that in the best fuckin' way, just trust me."

He puts pressure on my back, having me lie forward until my breasts rest against the still warm tank of his bike. I'm curious what he plans to do. He probably should've taken my shorts off prior to me climbing on if he's going to have me from behind.

"What are you doing?" I mumble, laying my cheek on top of my fingers in case there's grease or something on the tank.

"I'm taking care of you like I should've done the moment I saw you." His hands grip my hips, lifting them up until each of my thighs rest on top of his, and my ass is slightly elevated. "Hold still until I say otherwise."

"Why, what are you doing?"

"Just hold still or it'll hurt."

Well, that's reassuring.

Drawing in a deep breath, I hold it in, waiting for whatever he's about to put me through. There's no telling, but when it comes down to it, I trust him. Something cold and metal touches the inside of my thigh, kind of like a cool pen tip. He moves it more forcefully, a ripping sound happening along with air finding places it previously couldn't get to. It takes an abundant amount of control for me to hold still and not freak the hell out as I finally come to the conclusion that he's using his large hunting knife between my thighs, sawing away at a pair of my favorite shorts.

"I could have taken them off," I whisper.

"Shhh, Cinderella. This way I get to that dripping wet cunt, and I also get to play with my favorite knife." Once he slices through my shorts completely, he pushes the material up, leaving my ass cheeks on display in the moonlight.

Viking jostles around some, his belt clinking as he unbuttons the buckle and pushes down his pants zipper. After a few moments, he adjusts my body more, having me scoot farther up his bike. Gripping my hips, he moves me until my lace covered pussy is pressed deliciously against the small part of the tank.

Two of his fingers trace the scrap of material barely covering my core, eventually pushing it off to the side. The brief rubbing he rewards me with is enough to have me squirming and forgetting all about his blade previously being there. One moment Viking's pressing his palm against my needy center tantalizing me further and the next he's entering me without a warning. His cock so full and thick, stretching me to the ideal point, right on the edge of pain.

"Ohhh!" A whimper quickly transforms into a moan of pleasure as I close my eyes, reminiscing in the sensations.

He palms my ass cheek with his giant paw, squeezing it roughly and thrusting again, deeper this time. He's long enough that his dick hits all the right places inside, making you wish it'd never stop. Viking's not the kind of man who hesitates; he dives right in. It may hurt some in the beginning, but then it'll morph into a crazy intense orgasm.

"Tell me," he gruffly commands.

"About what?"

"I want to hear how it was riding on the back of my bike."

"Scary at first." Gasping, I hold on tighter to the cool handle bars while he drives in, the action causing my nipples to graze the hard surface deliciously. "But when you changed gears, it felt so good."

"Yeah? That why your cunt's so wet?"

"Yes."

"Good. You know what I'm going to make you do?"

"Huh?"

"I'm going to pump your pink pussy full of my cum, 'cause my Ol' Lady needs to have my seed in her every fucking day, marking her as mine."

"Uh huh," I manage breathily as he pulls my hips into him, seating himself to the hilt.

"Tonight, I'm taking away that little string you got on that you call panties, along with all your other clothes. The only way you're riding back is with that cunt pressed against my seat, wearing nothing but my T-shirt. I want your pussy juice spread all over it by the time we get back. Got it?"

"But what if there isn't enough?"

"I'll make you cream plenty," Viking grunts, leaning forward for smaller thrusts.

Too consumed by his demands, I'm busy imagining how it'll feel on the back of his bike with nothing filtering the pulses that'll be directly hitting my core. This time, I'll be wearing nothing but his shirt.

I don't notice him grab the handle bars. With a flick of his wrist, a strong vibration assaults my clit as he starts the motorcycle. The wondrous purr makes me scream in ecstasy. With each loud rev his bike makes, he plunges into my core, causing my greedy pussy to convulse. It feels beyond erotic, the sensations out of this world, taking Viking mere seconds to break my body down into a withering mess of multiple orgasms, milking his cock for whatever it'll give. One after another he commands my body to yield, spanking my bare flesh like a harsh kiss in the moonlight.

Viking bites and sucks, turning my skin tender by marking me anywhere he can get to in our position. The bar may have been a public claiming, but this is by far a private one with him bending my stubborn will into submission. With this sample of what he'll do to me, next time I'll cut to the chase and gladly beg.

After my third orgasm hits, stealing more of my energy, his movements begin to slow. Eventually, he stops and has me turn my body to face him. He spreads my thighs over him so I can sit comfortably and still be impaled with his cock.

Peeling my thin tank top off, I free my breasts, putting them on display. Viking is a full-on tit man and after giving me so many orgasms, he deserves to be rewarded. He takes my shirt from me, tossing it away from the bike and plants his palm on the back of my neck, gripping it with just enough force to warn me that he can take back control anytime he wants it.

His other arm gets braced across the top of my butt so I can hold on to one of his biceps. In smooth, fluid movements, Viking rocks me, slowly, back and forth, entranced, as he watches me. My eyes roll heavenward as my clit grinds into him each time my hips fall forward, making me clench my pussy muscles inside, eagerly anticipating a possible fourth orgasm.

This started out with him wanting to teach me a lesson for teasing him with my tits, which I'd say he's definitely accomplished. I'll be rubbing my body against his, anywhere we go, if it means he'll make me ride him and the bike at the same time again. I'm also curious now what make-up sex would be like if we were to really piss each other off somehow.

The claiming at the bar and then again later that night in the hotel was strictly Viking taking what he wanted. I get it, not that I understand it completely, but it did teach me right away not to expect anything average when it comes to this man. Bethany was right about one thing; I set the standard to a whole 'nother level with him. However, I wasn't expecting him to meet it and then raise mine as well. In the end, when the night was over, I had loved almost everything he'd done to me.

When I had time away and was able to start processing it all, I came to the conclusion that deep down, I believe he would have had me sooner or later whether I gave it up to him freely or not. It's terrifying when I think of someone obsessed and violent toward me like that. On the flip side, it's unbelievably empowering, knowing that he wants me badly enough to claim my mind, body, and freedom. To know that he's mine so completely, that he'd kill for me.

Having Viking like this tonight covered in someone else's blood—enraptured by me and my body—is different. At some point during everything, I surrendered myself and became his. He didn't take me for a test drive; he signed the fucking contract and demanded I give him everything.

Right now, this very moment, he's allowing me to ride his cock, on his motorcycle, while he wears his colors proudly. This is Viking surrendering to *me*. Tonight he's showing me that not only am I his Ol' Lady, but he's my Ol' Man.

And, for once, that doesn't seem so fucking bad.

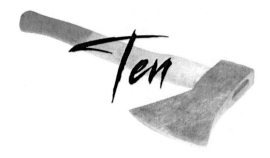

Ten

VIKING

Three days later…

"WHEN WILL YOU BE BACK?" I MUTTER, WATCHING AS MY Cinderella walks around the hotel room, collecting her things.

Tossing her lip gloss and brush in her purse, she shrugs. "I don't know. I can't keep calling into work, though; eventually, they'll fire me."

Doubtful. If they have any clue who her father is, she'll still have a job waiting. I'm not going to complain, though; I've had her at the motel with me for three nights in a row. She met me at the bar on Thursday and hadn't left since. It's Sunday now, so we've finally gotten some good time together.

"I got invited to a barbecue next Saturday. I want you with me."

Princess sets her bag on the bed, coming to stand in front of me. "Is this the same one those guys in the black car were talking about?"

"Yeah." *Does she realize Cain and Spin belong to her father's Charter? I should say something, but she's the one who shoulda' fessed up that Prez was her pops the same night we fucked.*

"I may have to work," she mumbles, glancing off to the side.

I know she's lying through her teeth and fuck if it doesn't make me want to hurt her for it. I hate feeling that way toward her, but I've cut men's tongues out for the same shit in the past.

"Ol 'Ladies are going to be there; you need to be on the back of my bike if I decide to roll up with my brothers."

Princess takes another step closer, her hands finding my hips as she presses her chest up against mine. "I'll see what I can do, okay?"

"Make it work." Grumbling, I graze my lips across hers in a peck. "Wanna have lunch before you take off?"

"Not today. I have to call my mom and Bethany as soon as I get home. We can during the week if you're not busy?"

"I said the barbecue is Saturday, not that I wasn't seeing you until then. I'll give you a night or two."

A beaming smile overtakes her mouth as she lets out a soft laugh. "You're going to show up and break my door down again?"

"Maybe, if I feel like it." My voice comes out raspy, as my lips brush against hers with each word.

"You're such a tease."

"Nah, I'm the real deal, sweetheart." Winking, I back away so she can get out the door without me taking her to bed for the second time this morning.

"So I should expect you Monday-ish?"

"Just expect me to be around anytime."

"You're really not going to give me twenty-four hours, are you?"

"You sayin' that like it's a bad thing. I thought bitches liked it when their man's up their shit twenty-four-seven?"

"I didn't mean it like that. Of course, I want to see you. I'm kinda sore though and was thinking about the downtime."

Letting loose a cocky chuckle, I'm beyond happy that I made her sore enough that her pussy needs a break.

"Just keeping my woman satisfied; can't have that juicy cunt needy."

She leans up, pecking my lips again, and then grabs her bag. "I'm going, thanks for the 'satisfying' experience," she cheekily replies, as she walks away, opening the door.

"I'll show you satisfying," I warn, striding toward her as she takes off outside in a rush. I easily catch up to her, popping her on her ass strong enough to make her let out a shriek of laughter.

Chuckling, I spin her around and push her against the car. Her face is completely lit up, a smile so wide it makes my lifeless heart skip a beat.

My mouth meets hers in a scorching kiss, the kind that has her wrapping her hands in my shirt, pulling me as close as possible, and about to climb my body by the time I'm finished with it.

"Holy shit, why do you have to kiss me like that when it's time for me to leave?" she asks breathlessly.

"Just owning that shit real quick so you remember it later."

"Consider it noted."

She pecks my lips again and hops in her car, rolling down the window and blaring her music.

"Bye guys!" she shouts, waving behind me as she backs out of the parking spot.

Turning back toward the motel, I'm met with Spider, Ruger, and Nightmare.

"Don't say shit." Grumbling, I shoot a glare at each of them, causing Spider and Ruger to grin.

Fuckers.

Heading back into the room, I grab up my wallet and slip on my boots. I'm starving, and since Cinderella had to bail, I'm going to find a big-ass burger. Making sure I've got everything, I head back to my bike, tying my black bandana on as I walk.

I barely mount my bike when Exterminator approaches. The other guys are suddenly nowhere to be found. I'm betting they heard us fooling around and came out just to be noisy.

"Ex." Nodding, I wait to put my helmet on to hear what he wants.

He stops next to me, resting his hands on his hips, appearing peeved about something. "We need to talk."

"All right; what's up?"

"A few brothers down the road need some shit."

So he wants me to run guns or narcotics most likely. It's not uncommon; we usually break off into smaller details. We're less likely to get picked apart by the cops if it's a few bikers versus a big group. If we're setting up a new business deal or handling blowback, then we take care of it as a pack.

"So what's the issue?" I don't like pussyfooting around; I prefer the facts, especially when it comes to the club's dealings. If he's pissed about a certain variable that has to do with our ride, he needs to tell me asap.

"Nothing, just ready for some new scenery. Scot wants to stay, so I'm heading up the run this time."

"We're all headed out, or just the two of us?"

"Everyone needs to be on this. I want to take off in thirty, so be ready to split."

"You want to fill me in first on why it's taking all of us if we're only visiting a few brothers?"

Exterminator clenches his jaw, his mouth growing tight, not liking the fact that I'm questioning him. I don't give a fuck about his feelings when it comes down to it. I need to find out how long we'll be gone to give Princess a heads-up.

The MC's top priority, but after laying claim, she's my first thought over club business. I don't want her thinking I'm taking off and not coming back. Her ass is already stubborn about being my Ol' Lady, and I can tell I'm finally wearing her down about it.

After a few seconds, he finally answers, "We're headed to Juarez."

"Mexico! What the hell do we have goin' on? I didn't think we had anyone down that way."

"We're making a quick exchange and getting the fuck outta there. Take extra ammo. You'll probably need it. I have to get the others." He finishes and walks toward Spider's room, cutting off any other possible questions I may have.

Fuck. Extra ammo? But yet it's a simple pick and drop? Doubtful. What the fuck am I gonna say to Princess, 'cause shit's about to get real.

Either Scot is getting serious about the bartender and wanting to settle in with the Chapter here, or this run is a shit storm, and Exterminator doesn't want us thinking about it with the ride ahead.

Either way, I can't help but think that I should have fucked my girl again before she left, 'cause you never know in this type of life if today will be your last. We don't have time to waste when you deal with scummy fucks on the regular; that's one reason why we're quick to claim a bitch and hope like fuck she's the one.

Is Cinderella the one for me? Just the fact that I'm even thinking about this shit and asking questions should be enough of a clue to let me know that she's got my dick on lockdown. She better get real comfy being my Ol' Lady, 'cause that bitch won't be getting another man until I'm rotting six feet under.

She handled the claiming, but can she handle the lifestyle that comes with it? I'm a fucking Nomad; she needs to come to terms that we work off my schedule, not one that some pussy-ass manager sets for her. One thing's for certain, when I return we're having a serious come to fuckin' Jesus moment when I lay it all out and clue her in. I'll set up roots and tie her ass up in a basement if I have to. I'm just fucking warped enough to do it too.

Digging my cell out, I pull up the finder app I have for Princess. Her mini crown blinks at her home address, showing me she hasn't gone anywhere else since she left here. *Good. I like when she stays home; then I know no assholes are hitting on her.* Closing it out, I bring up her number in the text.

ME: Hey, Cinderella, shit came up. I'll be with my brothers for a few days, maybe the whole week idk.

Closing the message out after I hit send, Sinner pulls up beside me. A large Taco Shop bag strapped under the convenient elastic net thing he made for his bike. Pretty fucking genius actually and the first time I'd ever seen it before. He took a car-sized trunk net you find that holds groceries and what not, customized it down to fit his bike and replaced the clasps with softer plastic hooks so it wouldn't damage the paint.

His engine quiets and he begins to climb off.

"You got any extra food in that bag?" I nod, as the delicious, spicy smell floats over, causing my stomach to growl.

"Yep. Exterminator hit me up a little while ago about the run. Made me crave tacos and figured half of you assholes would be hungry."

"That's what's up. Thanks, brother."

"No worries, I got you." He reaches in the bag, coming back with five wrapped tacos for me.

"Fuck, I'm starving," I mumble as he hands them over and I immediately unwrap a hard-shelled taco, shoving half of it in my mouth in one bite.

Sinner chuckles and shakes his head at me throwing a munch then strides over to Ruger's room. He beats on the door for a second, and when it finally opens, he's greeted with, "Hell yeah."

Guess I'm not the only one who was busy eating pussy for breakfast.

Later that day...

What should be a simple run down south, has morphed into a miserably long ride. The closer we get to the Texas/New Mexico border, the dryer the hot air becomes and even on a bike with the wind hitting full force, it does little to cool you down. I'm used to the humidity and have a rough enough time in central Texas with its smaller amounts of moisture. Down here the air is stale, making my skin feel dried out and filthy.

The sun's burned down on us the entire trip, thanks to Ex wanting to take off at a fucked up time. *Bastard.* This shit better be worth it. I don't bitch on runs. I love the road, but I would go fucking nuts it if I had to ride in this shit all year long.

Slowing, Exterminator signals and takes the off-ramp, leaving the highway that runs through El Paso. Right off the ramp, we're met with the entrance to the Mexican border. All the *You're now leaving the United States* signs they have posted does absolutely nothing to make me feel better. If anything, they make me want to tell Ex to fuck off about this run, but that's not how MC life works.

He picks a certain lane to go through, and we all follow suit, getting in line as a group. This could go down real fuckin' bad if they decide to search us. I'm packing like a motherfucker, and I'd put money on it that my brothers are loaded up to their ears with weapons and ammo as well. Princess will end up with a dose of reality if I have to call her ass from jail to bail me out or find me a decent lawyer.

The bikes rumble as we scoot forward slowly; it feels like it takes them forever to check through vehicles. The road and exhaust are making me stinky and sweaty. Nothing like being around a group of hot, tired, pissed off bikers. I'm thinking if we get flagged shit'll go down, border patrol agents or some ass-clown will get popped, and we'll all be shuffled to the pen on murder, accessory, and weapons charges.

Motherfucker.

Spider glances back at me, looking like he's going to upchuck. *Easy, Spidey, just stay cool and calm; hopefully, they'll let us pass.*

We can drop the majority of our ammo before heading back, so that's not the issue unless we're hauling something with us. Regardless, I'm not about to enter Mexico without packing some serious heat. I know a few brothers who've come to do a pickup and have wound up in a ditch, never seeing their home soil.

The cartel doesn't appreciate bikers on their turf who don't belong in their pockets. I've struggled too long to finally break away from pieces of shits like them, to be forced back under someone's thumb. Any of their minions or twisted pigs come at me, I'm shooting or scalping their asses, fuck the dumb shit.

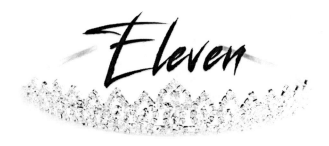

Eleven

PRINCESS

BETHANY PLOPS DOWN ON THE COUCH, PULLING MY PHONE out from the cushion beside her.

"Oh, my Gawd! I've been looking for that all freaking day." Hurrying toward her she hands it over, and I plug it in right away.

"I was beginning to think you were tied up and duct taped somewhere. Who goes three days without charging their phone?"

Setting it on the bar top, I impatiently wait until I can fire the screen on.

"I told you, Viking had me a little occupied. The phone wasn't on my radar when he was around."

"Then you lost it when you came home and ditched your shit all over the apartment like normal, yeah, but you didn't think to check the couch or behind the throw pillows?"

"You know I never sit on that couch; I checked the chair." The phone beeps with voicemails and text messages that I've missed. Once it's finished catching up and updating, I pull the notification bar down. "You called and texted me one hundred and fifty-seven times?"

"I told you! Duct tape!"

"You watch way too many movies if your mind automatically thinks that I'm being held against my will."

"Can you blame me? The last time I heard from you was Thursday when you were off to meet Viking at the bar. That's the same place where you were attacked and is always full of rebel bikers."

"Rebel bikers?" Laughing, I glance up to find her glaring.

Suppressing my smile, I try to make peace with my best friend. Who only knows what else was thinking up in that crazy mind of hers. "Okay, okay, I can understand your concern. I would have been as well if it were you."

"Exactly. Thank you."

"So what have you been up to then?"

"Well, I may have freaked out and stopped over at your mom's last night."

"Are you fucking with me right now?"

"No. I'm sorry! I wanted her to get your dad in case one of his bikers took off with you."

"Oh my God. I can't believe this. She's probably flipping out, calling in old favors." Scrolling through my missed texts, I scan for her number. She knows I hate talking on the phone a lot so she would have texted first.

"She didn't answer the door, so I never got to speak to her."

"Thank God. Never do that again. Unless I'm missing for like a week, then ask if she's seen me."

My eyes find one recent message marked 'Home.'

Home: Hey honey, just checking on my Princess. It's been too long, please come and visit. I miss you. I'm sorry that Dad answered the phone and upset you. We need to talk. Love you more- Mom

Reading her words, I can't stop from tearing up; it's like I can hear her saying them. *Damn it. I miss her.*

She was my freaking best friend growing up, not just my mom, but my everything. That's why this mission was so important, and I've done absolutely nothing but blow it. I needed to fuck a couple of asshole bikers and rub it into my father just enough that he would back off. I figured he'd be disgusted with me screwing his brothers that he'd leave mom alone for good.

I wonder if he's still at her house.

It doesn't matter anymore, at least not really. The mission's dead and over with. I found Viking, or well, he found me, I suppose. I don't even hate bikers anymore. This entire time I've been blaming them all for my father's faults. I don't want my dad hurting her anymore, but maybe Bethany's right and I need to back off. My mom's dealt with him for like thirty years or so.

I thought bikers were all bad, but they're not all selfish like my father. Viking's brothers seem nice and loyal. At the bar, they made sure I was safe and comfortable when he wasn't around.

Then yesterday we ate at the picnic table with Spider and Scot. Both guys were polite and funny the entire time. I enjoyed myself to where I was hoping we'd see them again. It was the total opposite of how I'd always thought bikers acted and treated people.

Was my mom lying? No, I can't go there. Dad seriously hurt her. I remember the days she'd lie in bed all day, face puffy from crying because he hadn't been home to see her, or he suddenly cut off contact. She never even went on a date with anyone else; I don't get it how she didn't eventually move on. The crazy thing is she's feistier than I am and she lets him treat her like this.

I remember one time we had to go up to my dad's old club. I think I was like eight years old. Anyhow, some woman kissed my dad in front of my mom. He pushed the lady away, but it didn't stop my mom. I remember my brother flying out of the car toward them and when I looked over my mom was straddling the woman just wailing on her. Once they were able to pull her off the lady, she slapped my dad in front of his brothers and then cried hysterically the entire drive home.

That time she stayed in her room for four days, only coming out to feed us until she felt better. No, she's not lying; I remember too much shit that happened. He's still the fuck up who screwed our family away.

I should call Brently this week. He needs to get the hell out of there and remember why we stayed away from Dad in the first place. I wonder if he's been to see Mom. That could be why she wants to talk and for me to visit. Dad probably left again, and she's going through her motions, alone.

"Yoo-hoo?" Bethany calls and I glance up, not paying attention to whatever she'd been saying. "Was the text that bad?"

A tear falls, my fingers swiping it away quickly. "Oh no, not at all. It's my mom; she wants me to come over."

"Are you going to?"

"Probably, let me call her really quickly. Do you mind?"

"Of course not; you know I love your mom."

Backing out of her message, Viking's name is next.

"Shit," I mutter with my gaze trained on his message.

"What happened? You haven't even dialed."

"No, yeah, I know. I was shitting because Viking had to leave town but doesn't know when he'll be back. He thinks a few days."

"Did he say where he was going?"

"Nope, bikers don't tell you that stuff."

"What the hell? He could have a wife and kids shacked up somewhere, and you'd never know."

"No, he doesn't," I defend automatically.

"How would you know? Think about it Princess."

"I have and well...When he was sleeping, I went through his phone and wallet." When I don't turn my back to her quick enough, I see her mouth drop open at my confession.

"You're so sneaky. Does he know? Do you think he'd actually have evidence on him?"

Grabbing an apple from the bowl using up a large portion of the counter, I take a hefty bite, starving with all the extracurricular activities I've been doing lately and face her again. "Fuck no, he doesn't know. He'd probably spank me until I couldn't sit down or something if he did; besides, this isn't CSI detective work or anything."

Her eyes light up at me implying he spanks, and I continue, "And yes, he would have something. I googled his home address. It was some little town in South Carolina. When I google mapped that shit and did a street view, it was an empty lot. It was literally grass and a mailbox."

"Geez, no wonder your phone died."

"Well yeah, plus I did reverse lookup on every phone number he had listed, which wasn't many, like fifteen."

"The next boyfriend I get, I'm calling you. How did I not know about this sneaky side of you? The one time we tried going out of your mom's house at night, you were so freaking noisy, she met us out back with a damn shotgun."

At that memory, I burst out laughing. Bethany eventually copies me, both of us giggling until my stomach starts to hurt.

"Oh God, I forgot about that! You were so scared I thought you were going to pee!"

"Yeah, pretty sure I did pee a little."

Laughter overtakes again, remembering her face and shriek when my mom scared the shit out of us, just waiting. It was like she'd already known it was going to happen and wanted to make sure we were so terrified, we'd never try it again. It definitely worked. We didn't attempt to sneak out from my house again—ever.

Once I'm able to catch my breath again, Bethany excuses herself to go to the bathroom, which ensures a few more chuckles, and then I bite the bullet and dial my mom.

I swear it feels like it rings for five minutes until the line's finally picked up.

"Yeah?"

Fuck. It's my dad.

VIKING

EXTERMINATOR HANDED OVER A NICE CHUNK OF CHEDDAR AT the border and was able to get us through without an inspection. I'm thankful, but where the hell did he come up with that cash? We haven't been paid in a while unless someone else gave him some paper up front for this run that's magically appeared out of thin air.

We ride for a while longer, eventually stopping in a small town called Calle De Norte. I haven't a clue what it means; I'm not Mexican. I'm gonna guess it's something North since we're fairly close to the United States, though.

Ex checks us in, coming out of the office with four room keys. "Bunk together." He grumbles, handing them out.

Ruger always eager for a job, speaks up, "Are we riding more tomorrow?"

"You saw that Compound we passed resting up on that hill about ten miles back?"

We all nod, paying attention.

"Well get some rest, 'cause behind that wall is men loaded with heat, not excited to see us."

He ends his explanation, unlocking his hotel room door. He opens it wide then comes back to roll his bike inside the room with him.

Nightmare shakes his head in Ex's wake, disappointed most likely because Exterminator's been cutting him out lately. They're usually boys and all that, as much as two fuckers who never speak can be anyhow. Now Night's left out in the cold with us other fuckers when it comes to information it looks like.

A worn out sigh leaves Sinner as he glances at Saint. "Want to lock the bikes up and head down to that bar we passed? We might find us a feisty senorita to share."

"I want some Mexican snatch and some tequila, but it'll have to wait 'til tomorrow. I'm goin' to rub my cock in the shower and pass out."

Sinner nods, fist bumping us as him and Saint trek to their room. Realistically they'll probably end up jacking each other's cocks off, but whatever floats their fucking boat I suppose.

Spider grins, "Not knocking on the old man, but I'm so glad I don't have to bunk with Scot tonight. He snores so damn loud and sleeps with his hairy ass hanging out."

Ruger and I both chuckle used to sharing a room.

"I need something to drink," Ruger announces, and Spider agrees.

"You two share then, I'm headed in now."

"Cool." Ruger nods and I pound Spider's knuckles, wheeling my bike into my room.

Nice. No sharing tonight. I don't mind bunking up, but privacy is even better.

Taking a quick, hot shower, I worry about getting the initial layer of road grime off and decide I'll do a better scrub in the morning. The main thing I'm wanting is sleep. My body is sore, and my ass is chapped from sweating all fucking day long, thanks to Ex's asshole move making us ride during the hottest part of the day. This run better be worth it with the vague answers and bullshit we're going through for it.

Lying down on top of the hard, cheap mattress I'm betting is full of shredded cardboard, I power my phone back on. I've learned being a Nomad and always on the road to keep it turned off when we're on a ride. Saves my battery, since I never know when I'll be able to plug it in.

The first thing that pops up is a message from my Cinderella, sent about four hours ago.

254-200-8699: No worries. I'll pick up some extra shifts to stay busy. Ride safe, and see you in a week or so. XO –P

Good girl. I can't help but think as I read it.

She may be Ol' Lady material after all.

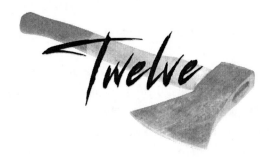

Twelve

VIKING

The next morning…

"I GOT SOME GRUB." SPIDER WALKS IN AS I'M PULLING MY boots on.

"From where?"

"The front desk told me about a little trailer down the way where you walk up to the window, just like a food truck." He chuckles, sitting on the opposite, still made-up bed.

"It's probably ground up cat," I remark, staring at the brown bag skeptically.

"You guys are so fucked up. First with Saint and Sinner talking about feisty senoritas and tequila and now with you saying these people are cooking cats."

"Nope, we're all just telling it like it is. Mexico has good, cheap tequila; of course, they want that shit. I may even take a bottle or two back with me, depending on the haul. They want Mexican snatch because they always want pussy wherever the fuck we go. As far as the food goes, did you see any fucking cats or dogs when we rolled through town?"

He thinks about it and remains quiet, proving my point.

"Exactly, now get your dick out of your ass and chill. You act like we're trying to fuck your mom or something. We're bikers, harden the fuck up."

He's the newest one to our group. I don't mind his company, but sometimes you can tell he's not like the rest of us.

"On the plus side, the food's only scrambled eggs in a tortilla. I watched them make it all."

"Thank fuck; I'm starving. How much did you get me?"

Digging through the bag he comes back with four wrapped burritos, they're thin, so I won't get full, but it'll work until later.

"Appreciate it."

"How's that app working?" he asks, ignoring my gratitude, like we all do to each other.

"It's on point. I've been tracking her every day she's not with me."

"I got an alert from your phone in the middle of the night, Saturday. She was clicking on each of your phone numbers and then I got a notification of her searching the numbers on her own phone's internet."

"It's freaky how you know all that shit. Did you block the internet searches?"

"I redirected them to random places you'd use, like a bike shop, a few Oath Keepers main club house numbers—that sort of thing."

"Good. I don't need her finding out my mom's info, thinking she'll be Suzy Homemaker and give her a call or something." I especially don't want her calling any of my old contacts. They're drug dealers and killers, not the type of people I want to know her name, even if they are friendlies.

"Nothing to worry about, you know I have your back."

Nightmare enters the room, not knocking as well. We're used to being in each other's space. "Ex is ready."

"Ex? You want to fill us in?" I ask and Nightmare sighs.

"No clue. I know as much shit as you. He's shut me out. Whatever this is, it's important to him."

"That's all I needed to know."

Spider wads up his trash, tossing it in the miniature bin and makes his way outside.

Nightmare turns to me, "He good?"

"Yeah, he's fine, starting to adjust."

"Bet. He's too smart with numbers and computers not to have him with us." His voice grows quiet as he finishes, "I figured out that's how Ex got money to pass through the border; he had Spider transfer rich fucks cash into a fake account."

"Serious?"

"As a fuckin' heart attack, brother. I don't know where the fuck his head's at, but we'll find out soon enough."

Nodding, I stand and roll my bike back outside, next to my brothers. We wait on Ex for a few minutes; eventually, he walks out as well pushing his bike and coming to stand with us.

"Here's the deal." He gazes over each of us. "This isn't a regular run. We're not here on drugs. Well, we are, but only if we find some, do we bring it back."

Sinner cocks his head to the side. "Then why we wasting our time?"

"We're not." Exterminator meets his stare. "We were hired by an undercover cop—a very rich cop—who's tied to the Russian Mafia. He's been searching for one woman in particular over the past months and got wind she was in that Compound we passed yesterday. He's paying us a fuck ton of money to obtain her."

Nightmare interrupts, "So you didn't have Spider steal money from a bank? Why didn't you tell us about this sooner?"

Spider coughs when he hears Night's conclusion and Ex growls angrily, "Fuck no, how well do you know me?"

Night cocks his eyebrow, and if either one's temper raises a notch, we're liable to be pulling them apart, or one would be setting the other on fire. They both have a fire and dumpster fetish.

"I didn't say anything sooner because the cop swears these people hear everything. He thinks that once he gets close to finding her, that whoever is keeping her moves her again."

"So we could be heading into a shit storm and not even come out with this bitch?" I mumble.

"Yeah, but we get paid either way."

And everything's right in the world for me again, knowing this is a paid job. Just wish he would have given us a heads-up sooner, especially communicating with a fucking cop. He better be careful. If one of the brothers thinks he's turned snitch, he'll never keep his spot in the club. He'll probably be strung up somewhere with a cord wrapped around his throat. We don't expend our skills on snitches; we just snuff them out as soon as possible to get them removed from the equation.

"We'll leave here and enter from the southeast corner. Satellite shows the least amount of guards and people in that area at all times. I have a general description of the female, but no one's seen her since she was a girl I guess. She's supposed to be a tall Russian woman, thin and she used to be blonde. They don't know if her hair will be changed, what language she'll speak, nothing. She'll most likely be one of the servants or maids. Let me know if you see one that looks Russian."

We all nod and mount our bikes as he does. Before we start them up, he shouts, "As soon as we have her, bail the fuck outta there, shoot whoever you need to and we ride toward the border as fast as possible. This is the Cartel, brothers; they won't fuck around."

We should've brought more men. Fuck!

With a sound like thunder, we crank over our engines, placing weapons wherever we need them for easy access and as one unit we hit the road, ready to piss off the fucking Mexican Cartel. We may as well be headed into a bee's nest because that's exactly how crazy shit's about to get.

PRINCESS

I STILL HAVEN'T SPOKEN TO MY MOM; I HUNG UP WHEN MY DAD answered. I don't know why he'd be answering her cell phone anyhow. Bethany comes out of my room, hair pointing in every possible direction and mascara all underneath her eyes. She stayed the night since I knew Viking wouldn't be stopping over at any given time. Knowing him if he shows up sometime with Bethany here, he'll demand to smell my pussy again. That man can be so flipping pushy.

"Morning, Sleeping Beauty."

"Ugh. That biker's already rubbing off on you."

"Huh?"

"With the nickname, I seriously doubt I resemble a Disney princess right now. I feel more like road kill."

"Well, you do kinda resemble a dead bird." Shrugging, I blow her a kiss.

"Shut up, some of us need sleep. Why are you up so early anyhow?" She passes me by, going straight to the fridge to get a glass of her favorite orange juice. I keep it around specifically for Bethany unless my brother stops over, then he'll drink it all just to screw with her. They've known each other far too long that they like to torture each other in small ways.

"Dude, it's noon."

Her eyes shoot to the clock, verifying the time. "Shit! I was out of it. I didn't pay attention to the clock in your room, with it dim in there; I figured it was pretty early."

"Nope, it's just cloudy out."

"That would explain why I'm starving then. Did you eat?"

"I had a banana, but I'm getting hungry now. Do you want to go somewhere or make something here?"

Finishing her juice, she rinses the cup and places it in the dishwasher. Stepping away from the counter, Bethany twists back suddenly, launching her face into the sink bowl. Fisting her messy hair in one hand, she braces with the other, wrenching up all the liquid she previously consumed.

"Holy shit!" Rushing over to check on her, I snatch a hand towel on my way. "Are you okay?"

"Ohhhh." She moans, expelling the water she had drunk before bed.

Flipping the faucet on beside her, I grab the sprayer, rinsing it down the garbage disposal, so she's not stuck looking at and smelling it.

After a few minutes of hovering over the basin, she wordlessly leans back, bracing both hands on the counter, staring at the drain.

"Bethany? Honey, you okay?" Cocking my head, I try to meet her eyes and push the kitchen towel in front of her. Her brow's dotted with perspiration but her skin's very pale.

She stays quiet washing her palms with soap, then takes the towel from my hand, never glancing up.

"How do you feel?"

Tears build up, running over her lids, flooding her cheeks with wetness, truly worrying me. I hate to see my best friend upset, so I lean in, wrapping my arms around her and place my forehead on the side of her head.

"Oh babe, don't worry. You can stay here and just lay in bed until you feel better. I'll make sure you have everything you need."

She breaks her silence as a sob bubbles up, and she finally faces me. "I need diapers," she cries, looking heartbroken.

"Okay, in any other circumstance, I'd give you *shit*," I giggle at the pun. "For the rest of your life, but I know you're actually sick. We'll just toss your undies out, and you can borrow a pair of boxers to wear."

Instead of laughing or chuckling, hell, even calling me a twat face like I'm expecting her to do, she busts out in a pathetic wail. I've known Bethany nearly my whole life, and I've never seen her like this—including bad breakups or drunken moments we've shared.

Bethany hiccups, her tearstained face swollen from crying, as I hug her to me tightly. Maybe we should go to the hospital if she's feeling this terrible. Shit, I hope whatever she has isn't contagious.

She takes a few deep breaths, her crying finally slowing down as she whispers, "I'm not sick; not technically, anyway. There's something wrong with me, though."

"What do you mean? Why haven't you told me sooner?"

"Because...I wasn't sure."

"You better not be fucking dying or something and just now telling me. I won't let it happen."

"I'm pregnant."

Shocked, I don't know if I should hug and congratulate her or cry, because in all honestly, there's a good chance she won't know who the father is. Her mom and stepdad will most likely kick her out even though she's an adult. They're dicks like that. She needs to find a better job so she can get her own place.

With my eyes wide, I mutter, "Wow."

"I know." She swipes her hand over her face, then fills a glass of water, chugging it down and refilling it.

"So that's what the puking was about and why you're suddenly drinking more water."

"Yep."

"Wow.

"You said that already."

"Who's the father?"

Grabbing the 409 from the opposite counter and a few paper towels, I spray the counter next to where Bethany puked. Once I'm done wiping it, she steps away so I can do the top of the sink. Coating the inside of the basin, I rinse it out and step back, still waiting for her to answer.

"B, do you know who the baby's dad is?"

"It doesn't matter, he doesn't want it, and I won't be letting him decide my child's fate. He's not the one carrying the kid around or who's going to be taking care of it, so it's not his decision to make."

"Holy shit, he doesn't want it?"

She shakes her head.

"What a dickhead; he should be castrated. Who is it?"

"I told you, I just want to forget about it. I have to figure out my life and how to support myself and a kid."

"Wait, is this the real reason why you called me so much and freaked out with Viking?"

Shrugging, she places her other cup in the dishwasher and runs her hands through her hair. "That's what started it, but then I did begin to worry about you when I didn't hear back."

"That makes sense. I'm sorry you've been going through these changes by yourself."

"Hey, at least I have you now. Plus, it's still too soon."

"What do you mean?"

"Well two days after I had sex, I was massively ill and went to the hospital; they couldn't find anything wrong with me, and then a nurse suggested that I could be pregnant. I thought she was crazy, but she said in certain cases a woman can be sick within days. She told me that my body may have registered the change immediately, where in others it takes longer to show pregnancy symptoms."

"That's crazy, so did they run a test?"

"Actually, I've had a fifteen-minute quick check with a nurse at my doctor's office daily since then. Yesterday before coming here, they ran a blood test, and it came back positive. My doctor was thrilled. I guess she's never had a pregnancy case like mine before."

"Why is that?"

"Well, because my test came back positive yesterday morning, making it eight days since I would have gotten knocked up. Today makes day nine. According to her, none of her patients have ever found out that quickly before. I have to go back in a few weeks for another test, but I'm convinced now after being sick every single day and then fine later in the day."

"I'm so sorry you've been sick. Is it that douche you were playing beer pong with, the night of the house party?"

"God, no!"

"But I haven't seen you go home with anyone else, except..."

Her head tilts as she nods sadly, "Nightmare."

"Ho-ly fuckballs."

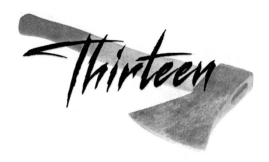

Thirteen

VIKING

MONDAY AND TUESDAY DRAG BY WITH NO LUCK ON breaching the Cartel's Compound. Princess hasn't contacted me again, and I don't know whether to be upset or impressed. She knows I'm with my brothers, and she's either keeping busy or letting me handle my shit.

I'm getting real sick of being here, though. I'm ready to slide deep inside my woman and eat a fucking burger. I thought the hotel mattress in Texas was shit, but it's a goddamn pillow top compared to the springy box I've been sleeping on here. It's going to be straight hell on us riding back, sore and grouchy, most likely with some runaway bitch while dodging bullets.

Now here we are, Wednesday morning and attempting to sneak in once again. We figured that if the place is usually loaded down with cartel thugs, then a quiet, early approach is probably best. The brothers are just as antsy as I am, ready to get the fuck away from here.

Ruger catches up to Spider, talking quietly, "Look, all I'm saying is, it's strange there isn't anyone in this part of the Compound. Where the fuck did they all go?" He gestures around us at the huge abandoned space as we continue our trek.

The back corner where we're located is littered with trees, a small brick building that we're assuming is storage, and random, massive-sized rocks, nearly the same height as me. It's weird, but who the fuck cares if it provides us some cover.

Shrugging, Spider glances around. "I showed you the satellite images. There were only a few heat signatures indicated with the program on the thermal mode. Unless they've decided to patrol, none of them are near this area."

Exterminator halts suddenly, whirling toward them. "Quiet the fuck down. This isn't school or some shit where you two can fuckin' gossip. If they hear us, they'll shoot. Now shut the fuck up," he orders.

They keep quiet, and we continue on our path toward a specific building Ex was told to search first.

Over the past two days, we've learned that the cop told Ex that he'd been watching the area closely and thought that this bitch he's looking for is being held in a certain spot. There are regular rotations that monitor it made by three guards at all times, which will be no biggie for us to overpower.

Spider had to wait until we penetrated the wall and were physically inside the cartel's perimeter to log into their camera feeds with his cell. Supposedly, whoever has this chick is insanely cautious and at any little glitch, he takes off with her and disappears. By waiting until we were on their land, the system they use wouldn't register it as an intruding device, just as one of their men trying to use the Wi-Fi. Fucking crazy shit that I'd never know about or even have a guess to think of; Spider's one smart little fucker.

Trailing along, I think of random shit, such as I'm grateful to have Spider with us and not against us. He's a good asset to have and will be even more valuable as he gets in more time on the road with us. I should have him set up some type of security over at Princess' apartment. I hadn't seen a keypad by the door when I'd left her place last week.

Sinner gasps, "You've gotta be fuckin' with me." He clears his throat as his steps falter. "Brothers, stop." He gazes around out in the field.

I don't know if he found an IED or a mine or what the fuck, so I stop straightaway. My gaze scans over the ground around us. With it being the Cartel, it could be absolutely anything. If it's not some explosive or drug, it's most likely a pile of dead bodies stacked up somewhere.

Next, Saint whispers, "*No.*" And we're all silent enough to hear it loud and clear. "Holy fuck."

"What?" Ex grumbles and Sinner nods to the open space off to the left side.

Everyone's eyes immediately shoot in that direction, concentrating to peer closely enough and pick out whatever Saint and Sinner have discovered. Personally, I'm looking for snipers. I wouldn't be surprised if they position a few out here to pick off intruders. It would explain the lack of heat signatures the guys were talking about earlier.

The choking sound that leaves Spider as he finally sees them doesn't surprise me one bit. I'd probably choke also...if I could speak or even move my mouth.

Nightmare grumbles, "What the hell we supposed to do?"

"Anything to the right?" Ex whispers.

"When I looked at the map I saw a small cluster of buildings. I don't know what they house, though, could be guard quarters."

"Do we run?" Saint asks.

"If it's a nest for the sentries they'll shoot us on site."

Finally, able to conjure up words, I hiss, "Better than getting eaten by two fucking lions!"

Glaring at Spider and Ruger, I point at them heatedly, "Remind me to fucking skin your asses when this is over with."

Spider's eyebrows shoot up. "I swear we had no idea."

My fingers find the snap securing the large hunting knife to my belt. Pulling the button free, I grab my knife and clutch it in my left hand. My digits go to the clasp holding my hatchet, drawing it free as well; I grasp it tightly in my right hand. I'm as ready as can be if those scary motherfuckers come at me.

I'll most likely die, but I'll be taking some of their blood with me.

The brothers all follow my example, preparing. Saint reaches around to dig in his backpack, arming himself with a machete. He passes another to Sinner. The others remove various weapons they're skilled with, watching the lions closely.

They may be lying out there, looking harmless now, but they can easily outrun any of us if they're hungry enough.

Exterminator murmurs, "Back up slowly, one step at a time, stay as quiet as possible. Think of them as bears. Ruger, keep an eye on where we came from. Night, watch the path that we were goin'. Saint and Sinner, you got behind us. Viking, want your eyes on those cats. You're probably the most skilled motherfucker out here with those weapons, who has a chance in hell at killing a goddamn lion. I'll be monitoring them as well. If any one of us is gonna die, it'll be me, not my brothers."

I've held a sense of respect toward Exterminator since the day he saved my life. He earned that, but today I respect him for an entirely different reason. The fact he'll put his life in front of ours speaks of true loyalty and brotherhood. This is why we look to him as one of our leaders; he's willing to ransom himself before us and take responsibility. I won't argue with him, but if it comes to it, I'll be the one forfeiting my life so he may live. I owe him that, and I will pay my debt if needed.

We slowly begin stepping backward, steadily peering over at the enormous beasts, and it hits me that I should confess my initial intentions. That way they'll all hate me and not interfere when I need to sacrifice myself. The brothers in the Nomads have become my family over the past few years; I won't allow this to be their parting fate.

"That day, you showed up early and saved my life," I begin.

He cuts me off mid-sentence. "Why do you think I was early to the bar?"

"Because I'd been tracking you. I was there, waiting for you."

"Go on."

"I was sent to kill you from another MC, but you stepped in and stopped that rival club for me."

He grunts.

"You were the first brother to have my back, and you weren't even in the same club."

"You fuckin' proposing or some shit right now?"

"Just thanking you for offering me a new life."

I think it's the most serious conversation I've ever had with any of them. We don't do chats unless it's full of ribbing each other, planning club business, or discussing the best way to torture someone.

"You think we'd let you ride with us without knowing who the fuck you were?"

His statement surprises me, and I glance at him. He points straight ahead, ordering, "Eyes on the cats."

One of the lions decides that it's a good time to stretch, putting us more on edge as we keep shuffling backward.

"I know who the fuck you are or were. I chose that time to wait for you, knowing someone was tracking me. I found a young kid who had a shitty fuckin' deal handed to him and was following orders in place of the mercenary I was expecting. You've proved yourself to this club many times over; you fit with us. If this is your confession, I don't give a fuck about what it *was*. You're my brother, end of story. Now shut the fuck up, 'cause if those cats scratch me from you flapping your jaw, I'mma stab you in the same spot."

I would grin but watching the other lion stand as well, has my heart rate speeding up.

"Move brothers!" Ex growls and our steps speed up.

Sinner speaks up, "There's a chain link fence."

We all glance in that direction, finding that it's not any ordinary fence. I'd guess it to be at least twenty feet tall of heavy twelve inch wired squares.

Nightmare voices exactly what I was worrying about. "You better pray to whatever god you believe in, 'cause there's a good chance that fence is electric."

Both lions' heads snap to us, licking their chops and begin to stroll leisurely toward us.

"Oh fuck!" Spider says shakily, losing his shit and taking off, sprinting toward the fence.

The lions perk up at him running, crouching lower as they prepare for their next kill.

Ex catches on, realizing we've suddenly become more interesting to the felines, quickly becoming their next prey. "Beat feet for the fucking fence, now!"

Our steps thunder against the dirt, running full force toward the only salvation in site. If we get electrocuted, we may as well give up, 'cause we'd be well and truly fucked. I won't let that happen, though; I'll defend my brothers till my last breath.

Making it to the fence, everyone jumps, scaling our wire savior as quickly as possible. I know the lions run and chase us; I can feel the sturdy metal bounce and sway as they jump after each one of us.

As soon as I reach the top, I leap. Not giving a shit if it's fifty feet below me or twenty, it's better than getting a limb chewed off from trying to climb down the other side. Landing roughly on my hands and knees, I say a silent thank you in my mind. My fall could have been much worse, and I was fortunate this time.

Nightmare calls out, his voice laced with shock and pain. Snatching my weapons off the dirt near me, I immediately look for Night, ready to help him if needed. I find him lying on the ground at the base of the fence a ways down from me, clutching his calf.

Striding over to him, the lion roars next to us, busily pawing at the holes trying to reach us. The other one jumps again, scaling the fence a few squares up before it falls. It angrily roars at my brothers, pissed off that its dinner just escaped.

"What happened?

"Landed up against the fence and he got my leg before I could scoot away."

The cat growls at us.

Nightmare meets its primal stare. "Fuck you," he grits out, flipping the lion off.

"Can you walk?"

"Yeah, I need to wrap it, though. I can feel the blood runnin' down my leg, and the last thing I want is to attract more fuckin' animals." He shakes his head. "Of course, the Cartel would have wild fucking lions on their Compound. Makes perfect sense. I hope I see the motherfucker in charge, 'cause he's paying for this bullshit."

Chuckling, I cut the bottom of his pant leg. It's torn most of the length of his calf, but the very bottom is still sewn together. Parting the material, I discover a gaping hole. The lion didn't just scratch him; he tore a fucking chunk out of his leg.

"How's it look?" he mumbles, scanning our surroundings as I try to figure out how to fix him.

"You'll live brother, but you're right, we should tie it tight, in case there are dogs running around."

"Just fucking wonderful, thanks for that."

Taking my fresh bandana from my back pocket, I close the gash up as much as I can. Nightmare groans but holds steady as I snugly wrap the folded over material around his leg.

"Little tight, brother," he grumbles, wincing.

"Yeah, it'll fall off if not."

Liar. He seriously needs to be sewn up and who knows if the cut's deep enough to do permanent damage, but it'll bleed a shit ton if that wrap doesn't help out. I need to let Ex know.

We both stand him lightly on his injured leg.

"Someone should go with you back to the bikes."

"What? No. I'm no pussy-ass crybaby."

Shrugging, I drop it.

Sinner grumbles at Spider, "Thanks for that, dick. If you didn't take off, we could have had more time."

"That lion wasn't staring you down; he had me in his sights the entire time," Spidey defends.

Ex holds his hand up, telling them to stop. "Brothers, we need to find this bitch so we can split."

The guys nod, silently following Ex, hopefully in the right direction this time.

Fourteen

PRINCESS

BETHANY GLANCES OVER AT ME AS WE PULL ONTO THE SIDE road that leads to my mom's. "We're going to your old house?"

"Yeah. Every time I call my mom, Prez answers."

"So?"

"I want to talk to her!"

"He doesn't let you speak to her?"

"I always hang up."

"You're such an asshole. He's your dad, Prissy. You need to just accept it, that this is how their relationship is and move on."

"I get that and to an extent I agree with you, but what happens if she gets so fucked up sometime down the road from him leaving her again that she pops some pills or something and kills herself?"

Bethany doesn't answer, staring out the windshield as we near my mom's house.

"I refuse to feel like I stood by and did nothing. I don't have to go through with our plan by slamming the Prez in front of everyone, especially because it would now affect Viking as well. But at the same time, it doesn't mean that I have to like him or talk to him. Father or not, he left my life a long time ago."

"Look, I love Mona, I do; but that's not your responsibility. Your mom can decide to stop letting him around. Her actions aren't yours to own and neither should the consequences be."

"They may not be, but you tell me all the time, I have one mother and she loves me. I'm not going to stand by and not do something."

Pulling behind Mom's Impala, I shift my car into park. "Are you staying? Or do you want to come with me?"

"Isn't that Prez' bike?" She nods off to the side of my mom's car at the navy and black Harley Davidson Softail. Cost my brother almost twenty-four thousand dollars to take that bike home.

"No, the Softail is Brently's. I forgot you hadn't seen it yet." Gesturing to the side of the detached garage, I point out. "That's Prez's."

My dad's very picky about his bikes. He keeps them for years at a time, but when he gets a new one, it's completely different than the last every single time. This one's a Harley Davidson, Ape Hanger Custom, low-Softail Deluxe.

I have no clue how much he spent on it, but I'd guess a ton with its glossy black paint and silver pin striping. He'd never tell my mom anyhow. The one time he told her how much he had spent on a Harley, she flipped her shit. I remember hearing her say that they could put a kid through college, but he had bought a motorcycle instead.

"Crap, do you need me to come in? If you do, then I will; otherwise, I was going to wait here."

"No, it's fine, the pickup's gone, so they must've come and traded vehicles."

"Okay, will you leave the car on so I can listen to music?"

"Yeah, of course. I'll be right back."

Slamming my door, I follow along the narrow, worn grass path and hop up the steps to the porch. Stopping at the front door, I take in the aged dark gray paint. It's fading enough to make out the wood underneath, and it sort of makes me sad. We painted this door right before my dad finally left us. Now, like the paint, we're all worn down, a little vulnerable and exposed when it comes to outside elements.

Taking a deep breath, I twist the door handle; only it doesn't budge. *Okay then.* Pressing the door chime and folding my arms over my chest, I wait for her to answer. It feels as if five minutes pass with nothing, so I try knocking loudly.

She still doesn't answer, which is odd because my dad never takes her anywhere with him and her car's parked out front. *Maybe I should call.*

Jogging back to my car, Bethany turns to me as I slide into my seat.

"Everything go good?"

"She didn't answer; I'm going to try her cell."

Bethany nods and sits back as I dial.

It rings and rings, but she doesn't pick up. Her voicemail clicks on, which I never use, but decide to in this case. "Hey Mom, it's me. Umm, I stopped over, but no one answered, so I guess you're somewhere. I was hoping to talk to you about the guy I'm seeing. It's becoming serious, so...well, I was thinking of bringing him by sometime. He's... different. Anyhow, let me know what you think. Love you more," I finish and hang up.

"That sounded a little strained."

"It's just weird because we've been talking over random messages, nothing consistent like it used to be. I sort of feel like I have this new life, and she's not in it anymore. Ugh, I feel so shitty admitting that out loud."

"It'll all work out; just bring the big guy over with you sometime. She's totally going to freak. You know that, right? He's pretty much everything you've fought against. Your dad's an alpha, in charge of all those guys, but Viking makes him look like a sweet old man. Not only that, but you're in love, and she's going to be so excited for you."

"I'm not in love." I turn the engine over, backing out. *It's too soon.*

"Please Ol' Lady; your ass is so in love." She rolls her eyes and no matter how much I don't want to, I laugh.

We head back to my apartment, and I swear to myself that I'm going to bring my Viking to meet her. She deserves to be included in my happiness, and I want my mom back.

VIKING

ANOTHER PINT-SIZED THUG CHARGES AT ME, AND I DRIVE MY blade into his chest, following up by swinging my hatchet into his kidney. It's messy, but it works. At this point of the trip, I'm done fucking around.

I don't know what the hell they're feeding these assholes down here, but they're goddamn runts compared to the brothers and me. It's not that I'm complaining, there's like twenty of them on us at a time. Not to mention they're loaded down with weapons and walkie-talkies to call for more backup. At least I figure that's what they're radioing for; I have no idea. Watch it be a tank or some shit. After the run-in with the lions, couldn't say it'd surprise me.

Shorty drops to the ground, gurgling in agony as he bleeds out. One of his buddies runs at me, and then falls flat on his ass when I extend my leg, getting him with a strong kick to the ribs. He gasps, attempting to catch his breath as I stride over to him and finish him off with a few swift kicks to his skull. Size fourteen, steel toed boots will do some serious damage when properly executed.

"Stupid fucker." Grumbling, I shake my head at the two dead idiots at my feet. "Drink a damn protein shake next time."

Saint steps beside me, covered in blood.

"Looks like you were playing with your food again."

He smiles widely, and then let's loose a loud, wicked laugh. "Hell yes, you know I like them bloody! Oh and Ex wants us to keep moving; he said to hit up the shed on the left. They're checking the right, and then we need to meet back behind our building in case we need some cover."

Nodding, I take the lead toward the small shack.

This place is trippy; it's littered with these random square structures built out of cinder blocks. Reminds me of something you'd see when building a basement. Each has a steel door with a padlock holding it closed and one window covered in bars. I don't know if they were making temporary cells to sort drugs or what.

Part of me's a little hesitant to open them, knowing they've kidnapped people and shit. I swear if I open one and find a kid that's been fucked up, I'm liable to go Rambo on every motherfucker here, taking them all out.

Saint digs through his rucksack again, coming back with some sturdy metal cutters. It takes him seconds to get the cheap lock off and step to the side. Putting everything away, he replaces it with his fully-automatic Glock Eighteen with a silencer. Once he's ready, he nods.

Heaving the thick metal open, Saint points his weapon, ready to shoot any potential threats.

"Fuck," I mutter out with a sigh.

"Holy shit, that's all heroin?"

"Looks like it. Ex said we could bring some shit back with us if we had time, but I'm not running no fuckin' H."

"I have lighter fluid; we could try torching the place after we find the Russian."

"Sounds good to me."

Closing the door behind us, we silently creep around the back and wait for everyone else to meet up so we can go over the rest of the plan.

Leaning against the building, Saint glances over at me. "You talk to your Ol' Lady?"

"Not today. What's it to you?"

"Nothin' brother, but bitches like it when you call them every day and text them pictures."

"Thanks for that life changing advice you just shared with me; I'm fucking touched."

He chuckles, "Just trying to give you a one up on keeping her locked down and all."

"Cinderella knows better than to pull any drama bullshit with me, making demands and what the fuck ever else chicks try to do. She's not going anywhere."

He shakes his head. "You think she's submissive and always gonna do what you want, but you're wrong. She's fucking smart, bro; she's an observer, like Sinner. He met her at the door the other night when she came to the bar. Didn't say two words to a soul all night; anyone else would've thought she wasn't paying attention, but I watched her the entire time. She has that same mask her father does; you can't read her. She only lets you see what she wants you to. At the very end of the night, she mutters out a few words about you, brutally fucking honest. I think a few brothers damn near choked when they heard her speak and not to give a fuck whether we agreed or not. She's got strength. She might let you think she's pliable, but I'm warnin' you, stay on your fuckin' toes, 'cause better believe she's gonna keep you on them."

After his big spiel, I'm stunned. How the hell did he get all that about her, but I haven't and I've spent the most time with her over anyone else? I know Cinderella's smart; it's one of the many things I find hot as fuck about her. *But* I also thought she was just naturally more of a quiet person like me.

I can see her being observant. He's also right that I do believe she's submissive. She could be a natural sexual submissive but not in another part of life. It would explain a lot. Not that I give her much of a choice, anyhow; I'm dominant. I've known it since the first female I fucked. Hell, even the first one I kissed, ended with me controlling it.

"I'll give it some thought. I'm fucking surprised you got all that."

He shrugs. "I have a lot of experience with chicks."

Pulling my phone out, I check to see if there's anything from her, but my screen's blank. I start to put it away but think of his advice.

Me: I may make it back by dinner. Fingers crossed. Be ready.

That sounds good and to the point, so I hit send and start to stuff it in my pocket when it vibrates. Immediately I draw in a breath, excited she replied so fast. Clicking the message icon, it's some shit telling me that the message wasn't sent.

I start to retype it when Sinner rounds the corner. Saint and I jump from leaning against the building, having relaxed our backs against the cool blocks in the shade. Holding the power button, the cell turns back off, and I stuff it in my pocket.

Sinner rests his hand on the shoulder of a dark haired woman, walking her forward.

"Who the fuck's this?" I mumble, scanning her over.

"She was one of them cleaning. Ex said if we found any of the maids that they may be able to give us intel."

"Where's everyone else?"

"They're still in the main house searching."

Saint gapes. "We were supposed to check the small buildings, not the main house. You should've waited for me."

"I'm straight; they had my six," Sinner replies, pushing the lady's back against the wall, so she's facing us all. "Should we question her now, or wait for the brothers to get done?"

"Ex has the most info, so let's just wait for him."

They both agree, and we grow silent, all staring at the maid, curiously. She must be used to strange men watching her because she stands still, not cowering into herself. Most women put on display to three huge guys would be scared out of their minds. This one's calm, like it's a normal occurrence.

Male shouts followed by multiple guns firing ring out, putting us on alarm. Saint peeks around the corner to see what's happening.

"Shit," he mutters, glancing back at us. "The brothers are running toward us."

Suddenly they go flying by, Nightmare shouting, "Get the fuck outta here! Come on!"

"You want her?" I ask Sinner.

"Hell yes, she could be our only hope."

Snatching her away from the wall, I toss her over my shoulder in a fireman's carry and take off after the guys. Saint and Sinner flank me on each side, shooting while I concentrate on not losing the maid as she bounces along.

Arriving at the outer property wall, we're trapped inside if we don't go over the fence and into the lion's den again.

"The fuck we gonna do now?" Ruger huffs, staring down the solid barrier that's keeping us from our freedom.

"Follow my lead, keep your gun on you and shoot anything that moves too close."

I don't see any lions chilling anywhere, so I start climbing as quickly as possible. Eventually getting high enough to reach the top of the wall, I move my body until I'm lying on the ledge looking down on the other side.

Spider shouts for the other brothers to hurry up and climb faster because the cartel guys are catching up.

"This is gonna hurt," I mutter to the maid and push her off me.

She flies through the air, quickly meeting the hard ground with a yelp. Launching myself off afterward, I try to position how to land somewhat decently since I already know what to expect from earlier. The maid's obviously scared now as she silently cries, not looking at me but it's no love lost on my part. She's lucky I didn't drop her ass in with the lions on accident.

The brothers start jumping from the wall and as they land we help each other up, waiting until the last one's over, and then make a run for our bikes. We're about halfway to our freedom when we hear a surprisingly loud roar. Casting a glance back, while keeping my pace, I watch as a lion rips into one of the Cartel guys who'd just hit the ground. Two men sprint, taking off toward the front of the Compound and the other lion gives chase, eventually jumping on them and brutally attacking as they scream in agony.

"The wall!" I gasp as we reach our rides.

We'd blown a huge fucking hole into the barrier where we'd broken in. At the time, though, we had no idea it led inside a makeshift den. It looks like we unknowingly granted their freedom as well.

Nightmare cocks an eyebrow. "I think those fuckers trying to kill us, unintentionally saved our lives."

Ex barks, "Sinner, have the bitch ride back with you." Then he starts his engine with us following suit.

It's clear by Sinner's pissed off expression that he's not happy getting tasked with babysitter duties, but he's the one who found her after all. I never get a chance to text Princess as we race off in the early morning air. It's barely seven a.m., and we've already been through enough hell for the day.

At least I get to see my woman tonight. She'll make the eleven-hour ride completely worth it.

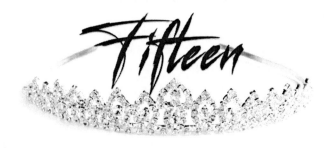

Fifteen

PRINCESS

IT'S BEEN A FEW DAYS SINCE I RECEIVED THE TEXT FROM Viking letting me know that he was going out of town, so imagine my surprise when my phone rings and of all people, it's Scot calling me.

Immediately, I spaz out, jumping to conclusions that Viking was dead, and Scot, being the one semi in charge, was calling to tell me about it. Talk about overreacting. Bethany's baby news has had me on pins and needles, automatically jumping to wild conclusions on everything, even the small stuff.

The poor man barely got three words in before I was peppering him with questions about why and how it happened. Chuckling loudly, he'd ignored my craziness and told me that it would be a cold day in hell when someone was able to kill that rotten bastard.

I'm not one hundred percent sure what Scot meant by that exactly, but it did indicate that Viking was okay. Bethany's words sunk in a smidge more, suggesting that I do love him. It's the first time as his Ol' Lady I guess you'd say, that he's on a run, so I can't help the nervousness bubbling up inside.

Scot was nice enough to let me know that they'd all be returning from their trip this evening, and he was hoping Bethany and I would go to the bar early and help the bartender prepare. Of course, I agreed, eager at the chance of possibly seeing Viking early. Plus, I'd get to do something nice for him and his brothers. They've been kind to me each time we've seen one another, so hopefully, the culinary skills I've learned from my mom will further win them over.

It's much easier for me to keep Viking at some distance if people are around versus being with him alone. I want to be with him a little too much, and that feeling scares me. I refuse to be left home all the time just because I'm an Ol' Lady. I won't let him treat me like my dad did with my mother and with how strongly I feel about him already, he could end up doing that if he wanted.

Per Scot's request, the majority of my day was spent preparing my mom's potato salad recipe and chocolate cupcakes with chocolate frosting. I tried to bribe Bethany to come with me, but she had to work and wouldn't call in sick. I can't blame her. I'm proud of her for turning me down; she has a kid to think about now.

After the food was finished and I'd taken a shower, I found a cute outfit consisting of a thin tank and jean shorts, then I loaded my car up and headed straight to the bar.

1 Hour later...

Dutifully, I've been getting everything set up and ready with the bartender ever since I crossed the threshold. This woman is a workhorse; I'd never guess she could pull this much off with so little notice. I'd think she'd be exhausted from closing the bar down each night and would sleep all day long too. At least that's what I would do.

That's probably why she's been quiet. I hate not knowing her name, but she didn't mention it earlier, and I don't want to guess and fuck it up. She hasn't been rude or anything, but besides asking me to set stuff in certain places or help her move the long table, she hasn't really spoken to me. I'm too used to having Bethany chatting my ears off when we're together that being around quiet females gives me too much time to think.

Hopefully, these bikers are starving; otherwise, I don't know who's going to eat all this food. So far we've got a buffet style table set up full of fried chicken, corn on the cob, potato salad, cupcakes, rolls, grilled chicken and pineapple kabob's, chips, dip, and banana bread. She had some serious help cooking, or else I need to step up my game when it comes to the kitchen.

"Will you hand me that bucket? I need to fill the ice bins back here." She points to a gray bucket beside the table. She used it to fill a few large bowls with ice to set under the salads so they'd stay cool.

"Sure." I place the plastic forks down and grab the bucket.

Handing it over the bar, she smiles friendly and uses both hands to take it from me. "Thanks."

"No problem," I respond just as the bar door swings open, letting in a burst of late afternoon sunlight. Normally the place would've opened hours ago and been busy with the regulars, but she posted a sign earlier saying the bar's closed for a private party. The guys have no idea about it either. Scot's supposed to be calling them later on, once we're all ready and let them know to come on over. I hope it's a surprise they'll be happy about with tons of food and alcohol.

My gaze is instantly glued to the entrance, waiting for *him* to cross the threshold because I know when I see him again I won't be able to breathe. That's what Viking does to me; he steals my breath away easily with his crazy demands and no-holds-barred way of living. He orders me around like he's lost his fucking mind and doesn't think twice about me standing up to him. He doesn't care about anyone else's opinions; he does whatever he wants, and it's fucking liberating.

A rough group of bikers enters the empty bar, and my stomach instantly tenses. I've never seen them around here before. My mother made sure I was pretty familiar with the clubs in the Austin area. She wanted to be certain I knew which ones were friendly with the Oath Keepers if there ever came a time that I needed someone else's help.

Pretty sure that time is now.

The intruders' cuts advertise one percenter patches, and when the last burly man turns around to shut the door, I make out 'South Carolina' on his bottom rocker. He swings back before I get a chance to see exactly which club they're from. The fronts of their cuts have each of their road names, the percenter patch and various other warnings sewn on, but no club name.

Damn. I need one of them to turn again; their name could mean so much.

My mother had also taught me about the types of patches that they sew on their cuts and what all they imply. I can tell you right now, these guys are at least into guns and drugs, possibly prostitution as well. It looks like they've all killed before, every one of them. A few have knife patches, and others have stripes marking their kills.

The two cuts with the tally mark patches most likely mean that those men are the club's Enforcers. Paired up with everything else they have on display, they're probably very mean bikers, taking care of the unwanted stuff thrown at their club. One approaches me, hardened features, glaring coldly like he wants to stab my eyes out.

His expression has me throwing on my resting bitch face. I'm pretty good at coming off to guys that I'm not interested or that I don't care about anything they may say. My gaze shoots to his title, reading 'Death Dealer.' *Definitely a damn Enforcer. Shit, fuck.* Whatever the reason is that they're here, it probably isn't good news.

With a road name like Torch, I'd hate to be on the receiving end of his anger. Thankfully, he keeps walking, heading toward the bathrooms.

The oldest guy with them spots me right away, and his eyes sparkle in triumph as he saunters toward me, wearing a malicious smile.

Just great. My stomach churns, knowing inside that this isn't going to end well. *Why can't these assholes just read the sign on the door and leave?*

"Well, well, well, looky here, Widows!" he announces as he comes to stand in front of me.

I'm not going to lie; I kind of want to shit my pants right now. This man is damn near as big as Viking; only he's scary as fuck. When I look at Vike, I see a man that worships me. This guy seems more like he wants to peel my skin off and wear it. Most men I come across are overly sweet, trying to get into my pants; but clearly, these guys don't use those tactics.

A skinny cracked out looking guy with greasy black hair snickers as he swaggers closer. "Nice. Her tits are bigger than the picture."

Any other time, I'd flip him off and tell him to lick shit off a toilet, but one thing stands out in my mind. He said 'the picture' as if he's seen me before and already knows who I am. It's like setting off a shrill siren or lighting a blazing fire directly in front of me—the warning written in his words.

My gut was right to feel uneasy; it was cautioning me that these men will hurt me.

Swallowing down my fear, my thoughts race to find a way out of this situation. I could try to make it out the side door, but most likely they won't let me back there alone, and if they did, then it most likely means that they have someone waiting outside.

Shit fuck. Could this be my father's fault? Did his damn club get mixed up in something bad enough that people would come for me? It's not a farfetched thought; it wouldn't be the first time.

Back when I was seventeen, I was leaving the movie theater and was left alone out front. My friend's boyfriend gave her a ride home, and she had taken off before my brother showed up. A rival club member of my dad's happened to be there, taking his Ol' Lady to a movie as well. They saw me waiting to leave and tried stuffing me into their old beat-up pickup truck.

Thank God my brother showed up just in time with a few of his college buddies or who knows what could have happened to me. My mom flipped out, scared for me to go anywhere alone and ripped my dad a new one. Come to find out, the other club had been threatening my dad for some time because one of his old members kept stealing the other club's drugs. The member got kicked out of the club and my dad made as much peace with the rivals as fifty thousand dollars would buy.

Then the Twisted Snakes came after Brently awhile back and nearly killed him, so why should I think that I'm exempt from such repercussions?

There's no way I can ask my mom for help with this. I have to figure out a way to call Viking. I don't want him to get hurt, but I think the Nomads are most likely the only ones who would be able to get me out of this situation right now.

If I don't do something fairly quick, I'll probably end up raped multiple times and then killed when they're all finished with me.

Viking's on my speed dial, but if I reach into my back pocket right away, I think the monstrous guy hovering over me will know exactly what I'm doing and take my cell from me. That's the last thing I want right now if I have any hope of making it out of this with minimal damage.

Clicking his tongue, the man looks me up and down. "Snatch got your tongue, baby?" He chuckles, and I clench my teeth together. I'm going to barf all over this jack off if he keeps talking to me like that.

Remaining silent, I mentally start slowly counting to ten, so that I don't come back with a retort that I'll end up regretting.

It takes no time at all for his weathered features to contort in anger at my silent defiance. His hand shoots out toward my face, his fingers digging into my cheeks as he pulls me in closer. Coppery flavor consumes my taste buds as my teeth sink into the soft flesh, carving out painful cuts inside my mouth.

Momentarily, I forget to breathe, in shock and in pain.

At his commanding voice, I draw in a few gulps of air, doing my best to concentrate on his words. "I asked you a motherfuckin' question. You don't open that cum guzzler real fast; I'll beat you 'til you feel chatty. You get me?"

Blinking a few times, I nod quickly, causing my teeth to slice in deeper where his fingers continue to hold my skin captive.

He sighs, and the anger melts away, almost like he just took off a mask and is a completely different person suddenly. His hand releases its fierce grip and falls away as a small grin appears. "Good, glad we understand one another."

Another man strides over, coming to stand beside my tormentor.

He resembles the older man slightly. This new guy's thinner but still muscular and young. I'd guess he's eighteen, if that. I wonder what could've been horrible enough in his life to make him want to be around someone so mean and just plain evil?

My gaze flutters over the man's cut in front of me; he wears the President patch on one side and his road name on the other. Jekyll. Taking in each material decorating his cut, one, in particular, scares me the most. It's actually more than one; there's an entire row of tiny red flowers sewn under his arm, all in a line.

Rape.

Those patches show me how many 'flowers' he's taken. I'm guessing he raped every single one of those virgins, as it looks like he's collected quite a few.

"You like those flowers?" he murmurs nastily, adjusting a little so I can get a better look.

Twenty-nine.

I'm able to get to number twenty-nine before he returns to his original position. That wasn't all of them either; that was just how fast I was able to count them. Shrugging, I pretend to be oblivious. Fake it till you make it, right? "I don't care for them."

Stepping closer, he places his finger in the 'v' where my thighs meet. "You sure?" He rubs my pussy through my shorts. "I could show you what they mean; then you could have your own. "He points to the last spot under the crimson line. "Right here."

"I'm not really a red person, more like pink."

He pushes against me hard enough to send an entirely new zing of sickness to my stomach. "I'll bet you are. Did my son get a flower patch from you?"

"Huh?" I'm confused. I have no clue who the hell this guy's son is unless he thinks I've met him before.

"Take off your shorts," he orders, causing me to panic. If I take them off, I lose access to my phone. *Fucking shit.*

"Not happening. I'm not some bar slut that you may be used to."

He snaps his fingers and instantly greasy hair guy along with another guy grab my arms, spreading them out. I can twist and turn, but they're strong enough, making it so that I can't go anywhere even if I do try to fight them.

Jekyll pulls the same long knife from his belt that Viking owns, wearing a cruel smile as he grabs my shirt, slicing up the thin tank top material. Once he has most of it cut away, he pulls the scraps off, tossing it to the floor.

I'm left in my bra, panting, my anxiety making me feel as if I'm about to have a heart attack. "You seriously need to stop; you don't know what you're doing!"

"That's where you're wrong. I'll do whatever the fuck I want, whenever the fuck I want to. You see this patch here." He points to the one percenter sign, and I nod, well aware of what it is. "Means, I make my own rules, and some snatch isn't gonna tell me what the fuck to do." He grabs my bra between my breasts; I try to wrench away, but they're too strong. I don't get back far enough, and when he slides the blade underneath to cut the bra, he draws my blood.

The sting to my sensitive skin is enough to have me spewing threats. "Do you have any clue who the hell my father is, you fuckwad?" I scream furiously. "He'll kill you! You're all fucking dead!"

Jekyll bursts out in a deep belly laugh, only pausing to send a quick punch to my stomach for my outburst. He hits me hard enough to make the air escape me, but not to break a rib. Watching me, he continues to chuckle for a moment while I gasp in discomfort.

The younger guy remains solemn, standing beside him and looking miserable like he's being forced to watch this.

"Blaze, come shut this mouthy whore up," Jekyll hollers at a stocky guy that has flames tattooed all over his arms.

Before he reaches me, I shout, "My father's the President of the Oath Keepers MC you fool! Let me go!" That's all that I can get out before Blaze is standing behind me with his huge hand, covering my mouth and muffling my shrieks of outrage.

"You think I don't know who the fuck you are, *Princess*?" He says it snidely, running the tip of the blade ever so lightly against the flesh of my exposed chest. I can't answer, just stand here helplessly and listen while my cheeks burn with anger and my gaze bristles with my newfound hatred for him.

"You're wrong. I know everything about you, where you live, your job, how long you've been sucking my son's cock, oh, and my favorite —the pictures from him fucking you right in this room on that pool table." He gestures to the old wooden billiards table with faded green felt.

He has no right to cheapen what happened on that table between Viking and me. He didn't just fuck me that night; Viking made me his. It wasn't some shitty show put on for the patrons like Jekyll's making it sound, what happened was carnal and raw. It was us.

Being a biker himself, Jekyll should know exactly what that entails. By the biker code, it means that if my Ol' Man shows up and witnesses what they're doing to me right now, he has every right to slaughter them without any repercussions coming to bite him in the ass. At this point, Viking could request the entire club to help him snuff out each one of the Widow Makers members in this room. Prez may be a shitty father, but he's always been one hell of a biker, and he'd be ballistic right now beside my man over this.

A shotgun loads in the background somewhere and then the bartender starts shouting, "Let her go and get the hell out, dickhead!"

Jekyll's head flies up with murder coating his irises toward her. He remains eerily silent, even as a shot rings out, followed by her pained scream.

Tearing up, I attempt to suppress the wetness from falling, but it's no use. I'm too irate at this point to not start crying. I'd use my anger by punching and screaming, fighting them, but they've stripped it away from me along with my modesty.

That woman was only trying to help me, and they shot her for it. These sick fucks are absolutely crazy. The only piece of comfort I find, out of everything, is that I can hear her crying. I can't stand it that she was injured because of me, but at least with her upset, I know she's not dead.

I'd give anything to be free right now and holding that knife in Jekyll's hand.

"Your father means nothing to me, same as you. I'll still fuck you and kill you when I'm finished, because let's face it, my son can't have an Oath Keepers dirty slut as his Ol' Lady."

My mind soaks up every word he speaks like a sponge, but my heart pleads with me not to listen. I don't want to believe anything Jekyll says, but he knows too much. I would be stupid to think he was lying and that there isn't a bit of truth to everything.

But how could Viking betray me like this? I was falling in love with him and now...Shit, fuck. Who am I kidding? I am so fucking in love with him, but there's no way I can be with him if he's going to be a part of this hateful club. The Oath Keepers will probably kill him for this anyhow.

Jekyll uses his free hand to twist my nipples painfully and sadly all I can do is whimper. I want to cry out, cursing him to hell, but I can't. At the strangled noise leaving me, he smirks, running his digits down my chest and stomach, pausing at the button on my shorts.

He leans in beside my ear, close enough that I can feel his short hot pants and pushes his fingers inside my bottoms, far enough to go under the elastic of my panties. "Let me fill you in, as I'm sure he didn't share the news with you," Jekyll mumbles quietly, "He's due to be patched as the President of the Widow Makers MC soon, and there's no way I'm letting you fuck it up. I'm ready to pass the gavel down and watch my oldest take my place."

No. Please be lying. I don't want him taken from my life. He's mine; he belongs to me. We haven't had enough time yet.

His calloused fingers rub back and forth over the smooth skin above my pubic hair, continuing, "He can have the gavel, and I'll have your snatch as my parting gift. You're one lucky little girl; in our club we share. Think of the fun you'll have being passed around until we dispose of your body."

Sickness whirls through me, my gaze blurring as my head becomes fuzzy and makes me want to wretch at the bitter flavor that's abruptly overtaken my taste buds. I'm confident and strongheaded, not letting people get me down in everyday life, but I've also been diagnosed with panic attacks. It was a wake-up call and also my doctor's way of telling me that I was trying to be too perfect for my father when I was younger. I wanted him to stay, so I tried everything I could think of, then he'd leave, and my mom would be a mess. I couldn't help but panic, and over the years, I've learned how to keep the attacks at bay by staying mad inside.

My anger's faded with Jekyll's torments, morphing into a sense of loss, fear, and sadness. His latest taunt has me conjuring up images filled with the room of filthy men sexually assaulting me and then killing me. Even with the air conditioner blasting cold air throughout the bar, beads of sweat trail down my back, catching on Blaze's shirt.

At the feeling of Blaze thickening and resting his cock against my back, shakes start to set in, racking my body with nervousness and fear. I can't stop the thoughts running through my mind that Blaze could easily rip my shorts down and force his hardness inside. *Viking won't want me.* More tears fall, and I gag into his palm, ready to empty the contents of my stomach.

Blaze's hand flies from my mouth like it's on fire, then sharp pricks of pain explode from my scalp as he grasps onto the back of my hair. Yanking the platinum strands harshly, he wrenches my head back in outrage. "You better not throw up on me, you dumb bitch." Growling, he shoves my head forward with such force, my neck pops, protesting the movement as he releases my hair.

Jekyll chuckles, amused at the display and steps back. "You can still have your turn whether she pukes or not." He's loving the fact that he's tormenting me enough to make me physically ill and that it's grossing Blaze out.

Blaze scoffs, "I'm not touching that twat if she's gonna fucking wretch. Maybe we should dope her up first. Besides, she looks like she's gonna pass the fuck out anyhow." He nods at me, and all the guys start to really stare at me.

"Well, I'll be damned, looks like Viking chose a weak-ass bitch," Jekyll chortles and the men all laugh in agreement. "Just throw the whore down, she can sit up against the bar. I don't want this one drugged up at first; I want to see if she'll try fighting me." They all chuckle again, and it takes everything in me not to toss my stomach contents.

The two bikers holding onto my arms drag me backward a few paces then propel me to the stained concrete floor.

My ass smarts as I land harshly on the solid ground, a smell yelp of "Shit!" escaping. Thankfully, no one pays me any mind because my cell phone digs into my butt cheek, reminding me of its presence.

A speck of hope rises, feeling the small square still in my possession.

Greasy guy crouches down, stopping about four inches in front of my face. Even with him this close to my nakedness, I can't help but pray silently that my screen isn't cracked, and I can get ahold of someone.

Smirking, he glances at my chest. "I'm fuckin' those titties when it's my turn." Flicking my nipple, he stands, staring at my breasts while adjusting what looks to be a tiny dick pressing against his dark wash jeans and turns around to face Jekyll.

Bastard.

He can think whatever he likes. As soon as I know that they're all distracted enough, and I get a chance, I'm calling for help. It's times like this that I'm my father's daughter, because when the anger comes, so does my clarity and I'm hoping that I get the opportunity to shoot this nasty monkey in his dick.

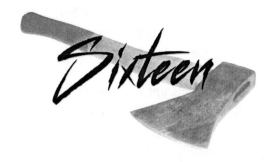

Sixteen

VIKING

WE ARRIVE BACK AT THE HOTEL AFTER A LONG-ASS RIDE and get settled in. We didn't speak two words climbing off our bikes, and I'm pretty sure the maid we brought along won't be able to walk for a week after a trip like that. I prefer the northern runs the most during this time of year, not this bullshit sweating until your nuts chafe, and you get a rash up your ass crack. It took me two showers to scrub the road grime off, and my balls are fucking tender enough that I'm not gonna be able to fuck my woman like I'd planned. It'll be slow and steady with her on top.

I'll give her a call shortly and head across the street for a beer to wait on her. I'm sure Exterminator hit up Scot and let him know we were headed back. I wonder if the old man knows what's up at the bar. There were about ten bikes parked out front when we rolled in. It's not unusual for the regulars to be drinking already; however, I didn't see any of theirs parked out front.

Nightmare had a hell of a time riding back. I'm thinking the heat and blood loss was making him weak after his adrenaline finally started to dissipate. At one point he was swerving so much, I thought he was going to pass the fuck out. I've never been worried about him like that. He's a tough dude, but I almost suggested he stop off at a hospital. I'm glad we were able to make it back first, that way no authorities will be flagged by him getting medical attention.

Heading outside, I check for him, but find his bike still gone. He decided to stop over at the Charter to see if they had a private doctor that'd look him over. Hopefully, Night gets that shit squared away; it would fucking blow if something serious happened to his leg because he was too stubborn to get it taken care of.

Digging a cigarette out, I get it lit and the first drag filling my lungs as Spider leaves his room. He starts my way, glancing up, surprised when he notices me already out here.

"Can I bum one?"

My eyebrow rises as I stare down at him. "It tastes like shit. Why you want to smoke?"

"Because I guess with how everything went down south, the Nomads are going to pummel my ass. Might as well pick up a bad habit on the way."

Chuckling, I shake my head, "Nope."

"No?"

"You a parrot now?"

"My bad, I'll ask the desk clerk," he says sincerely and begins to walk off.

"Spidey, get your ass back here."

Halting, he turns back looking like someone kicked his fucking cat.

"Look, brother; shit always goes down on runs. You're just too new to know that. Brush it the fuck off and if anyone gives you shit, just tell 'em to fuck off. Don't show yourself to everyone or they'll end up running your life. And don't start smoking, for the love of Christ; we've all been trying to stop since we started. Chew a piece of gum."

He nods, silently thinking it over.

"You still have your Smith and Wesson?" On our first run together we were transporting weapons, and Spider pretty much jizzed his pants when he saw a small, flat black gun we had in one of the containers. That was one business deal that went through flawlessly.

"Yeah, I've been getting familiar with it. The different design is sick, but I've also been looking into other models."

Exterminator rushes out of his room, beelining for mine. What the hell is going on with people today and coming to me?

"Ex?"

"We gotta talk—now!" He slams against my door, shoving it open swiftly. "You too, Spider," he orders and we shuffle in quickly. "You speak to your Ol' Lady?"

Meeting his stressed-out gaze, I shrug. "Not yet, my phone was off for the run, why?"

"Fuck, fuck, fuck," he mutters, his fingertips squeezing his forehead.

Grabbing my phone off the table, I power it on immediately.

"It's not good, Vike. You're gonna lose it, brother. You need to stay calm so we can figure out what the hell to do," he finishes as six missed calls from Princess pop up.

One voice message.

Clicking the message icon, I hear whispering at first, and then sobbing. My eyes fly to Ex's, just as she starts sobbing and pleading, "Please no, don't take it, nooo." Then the screaming sets in, "Viking help me! Please, they're gonna rap--" And then it cuts off.

I'm going to filet whoever did this.

Exterminator positions himself in front of the door with his palms out. "Calm down, brother. I just spoke to Scot. He heard from the Prez over here. Nancy, the bartender, called him asking for help too."

"Get the fuck outta my way!" Roaring, I charge toward him.

"Vike! Wait, man, we'll get her!"

Halting directly in front of him, I send him a dark glare. "Move." His eyes shine with sympathy which has me almost ballistic. "You wanna fuckin' die? Get the fuck out of my way, or so help me, I'll take your motherfuckin' life, Oath Keeper."

"It's the Widows."

The little bit of spit in my mouth damn near chokes me at that name. That's no regular MC; that's my *father's* club.

"We'll figure this out, what would they want with your woman?"

"He doesn't want Princess. It was my birthday yesterday; he's come for me."

"This isn't the way to get you a fuckin' cake." He shakes his head, trying to figure out what to say.

"Jekyll doesn't want to celebrate; he wants to give me the gavel. I'll get her back; if not, they'll kill her. She'll fucking hate me for what I'm going to have to do, but at least I'll know she's still breathing."

Spider interrupts, "What the hell, this isn't old England; you're not born into shit, you vote, especially on patches."

"True, but in the Widow Makers, you have to be a son to be the President, and if you live long enough for your first born to reach a certain age, then you inherit the gavel and the previous gets to hang his leathers, just ride free the rest of his days."

"So fucked up," he mutters.

"Yep. Now I gotta go save my bitch, 'cause I have a good idea of what they're doing to her and I have a plan."

"What is it?" Exterminator questions.

"I'm going to kill my father, and then I'll kill any other dumb motherfucker who steps in my way of saving my woman."

He steps aside, and I storm out the door, striding purposefully toward the bar.

"We're coming!" he calls from behind me.

"Give me twenty first and keep a look out for her," I yell back as I see the first Widow posted up by the front door.

A young member slouching against the building jumps to his feet quickly as I near. He must be a recent patch since I'm not familiar with him. I know all the lifers and members dating five years back. Most could be dead by now, but I doubt it—shady fuckers.

The punk steps to the top of the stairs, crossing his arms like he's king ding-a-ling. "Who are you?"

My steps don't miss a beat as I hop up the few steps and shoulder check his ass, causing him to fly back a few feet, landing harshly against the old wooden porch.

"I'm your new fucking President." Muttering, I pass him by and head inside the bar.

The sight I'm met with is sickening. My girl's on the floor against the bar, hair in every direction, halfway undressed sobbing as my father and cousin, Blaze, taunt her. She's got blood smeared over her tits and Butters' greasy ass is smashing her phone under his boot.

My father's in the middle of telling her how he's about to tie her to the bar and fuck her in front of everyone when the men quiet with me storming inside like a freight train.

"Son!" Jekyll shouts jovially.

Such a fucked-up man.

My entire life was lived on the edge, because when you have a father like Jekyll, you never know what's going to happen. One minute he's laughing and the next he's driving a knife into your stomach. Psycho is too tame of a word to fit him. He got his road name after Dr. Jekyll and Mr. Hyde. His father was proud of the fact he had a son that was off his fucking rocker.

I never use guns—ever. I'm strong enough of a man to kill with my two hands, but when I see Smokey's Glock out on the table, I don't hesitate and pick it up immediately, shooting my father in the head. Brain matter sprays behind him, and he falls like the dead weight he is.

One thing I'm learning about my woman is that I can't handle shit when it comes to her. My normal way of thinking goes out the window, and I become obsessed with her.

Obsessed with being inside her. Obsessed with keeping her safe. Obsessed with making her mine. Just fucking obsessed.

"Cinderella!" I demand, loudly.

Her tearstained face finds mine, and she lights up. *I love her. I will forever.*

"Get the fuck outta here. We don't have space for filthy fuckin' sluts." Nodding toward the door, I turn away to give her my back.

My younger brother stares at me in shock while my cousin Blaze comes toward me angrily. "You shot the Prez!" he accuses, and I cock my eyebrow at him, my nostrils flaring.

"Last I checked, yesterday was the fourth. That means this club belongs to me now."

Glancing around, the brother's nod, keeping their mouths shut. This is how it works. I'm in charge now, and they know that. I could have let my father live out a peaceful old life, but he would never have changed and seeing a drop of blood on my girl, he's lucky his death was swift.

Her grief-stricken voice rings out, causing me to spin back. "You bastard!" she practically wails, heartbroken.

Her palm stings as she slaps me with everything she's got. I don't get an odd punch from her somewhere; I get her 'in your face' disappointment launched at me, and I'll have to live with that moment for the rest of my life. If she only knew it was done because I want her to be happy and alive. I'll make these men believe I want her gone if it means it'll keep her safe.

A few of the brothers stride toward her, and I throw my hand up, halting them.

"Get the fuck out." Growling down at her, I point toward the door.

Her eyes refill with tears; sorrow swimming in them so deep that I feel like my heart's being cut out. In some ways I wish it were, I know it would hurt less than this moment. As she turns away, a noise close to thunder gets closer, and immediately I think of Widow Maker's reinforcers showing up.

"Princess, get back behind the bar," I demand, and sheactually listens right away.

"Who's that?" Butters, the dirty motherfucker, asks.

"You scared? Shut the fuck up."

"Maybe your poppa should've stayed longer," he utters, and I shoot him next.

"Shit, man!" Blaze yells as Butters hit the floor.

"I never liked him. Anyone else in here wishing Jekyll was still around?"

The room stays silent as the powerful rumble comes to a stop outside.

"Good."

"You've grown hard," Blaze notes.

"No. I've always been hard," I respond and point to my dead father on the floor. "He's gone. This club runs my way now. Anyone have a problem with that; there's the fuckin' door, and best believe shit's fucking changing."

My gaze lands on Odin, sitting quietly at a table. "Why'd he bring you?"

"Why do you think?" he questions back, standing and coming near. It's like looking in a mirror; only I had more bruises back then.

He's a big kid now. When I left, he was about to turn eleven. Now he's riding around with a group of outlaws at the age of fifteen. I can only imagine what kind of man he'll turn into if I'm unable to get him away from the bad.

"'Cause he was going to use you to get me home."

He nods.

"What'd he do to you?"

"Not me. He promised to hurt a friend of mine."

"Jesus fucking Christ."

Ex and my Nomad brothers storm in, guns drawn, ready to fuck some shit up. The resident Oath Keepers, including Princess' father, pours in behind them, and the Widows get to their feet, prepared for a fight.

"Stand down," I order. "These are my brothers, the Nomads, and this is the local Chapter of the Oath Keepers. They have my six and being your President, I'm telling you, we're cool with them."

Charlie stands up, his nine out in front as he grumbles, "Fuck this, we ain't friendly with nobody." He raises the weapon toward me, but my old best friend, Torch, steps out of the hall and shoots Charlie dead.

I didn't even know Torch was here.

"He brought you too?"

"Yep." He puts his gun back in his holster.

"What'd he do to you?"

"Threatened to rape my ex-wife and sister."

"Meggie?" I name his sister who's the probably the sweetest woman alive.

"Yep."

"That shit's fuckin' done. You won't be living like that anymore. We'll figure this shit out later, but your friends and families are safe, you have my word."

Odin scoffs, "Like that means anything."

"The fuck you just say?"

"You promised to protect me too. Next thing I know, you're leaving me in your exhaust. Whatever, I'm over it."

"We'll talk; that's not how it went down."

Prez comes over with Ares and Exterminator. "Everything okay, son?"

"We'll get it figured out. We need to have a meeting though to discuss the clubs."

"You're family; my door's always open for you," Prez answers, and we shake. I'm going to need his help with turning this club around, and he's one hell of a President when it comes to running a semi-clean MC.

The bartender and Princess stand slowly, looking around to make sure it's clear. My woman has a bar towel covering her naked chest, and being the overprotective fucker that I am; I want to gouge everyone's eyes out. Shedding my shirt, I swiftly help her into it and place my cut back on.

She doesn't look at me, but I can feel her physically move her body closer to mine.

Glancing around at everyone, I declare sternly, "This is my Ol' Lady. None of you better have touched her or ever touch her in the future. If I find out otherwise, my boy Saint will gladly hold you down so I can chop your fucking head off."

Blaze stares at the ground guiltily.

"Blaze?"

"I was keeping her quiet," he replies honestly.

Glancing at Princess, I ask her loud and clear, so everyone can hear me and know exactly where I stand. "He's my cousin, but I will kill him for putting his hands on my woman. You want him dead, Cinderella?"

She looks over at him, her backbone a little straighter with me beside her.

"I swear I will protect you with my life." Blaze meets her gaze, pledging his loyalty.

She glances up to me. "No, as long as he doesn't touch me, we'll be okay."

Smokey grumbles, "So bitches are choosing our fates now? You told her to get the fuck out earlier."

"Yeah, I sure the fuck did. I didn't know who the hell was here or if anyone had hurt her. I wanted her to get out so I'd know she was safe, with my brothers." I nod to the Nomads standing closer to the door.

"As for being a fate-maker, best believe you decide your own. You touch my property; I take your fucking head. Don't test me when it comes to her. You need to realize right here, that this is your President's Ol' Lady. You call her Princess or Cinderella. Anything else, derogatory or sweet, will get you fucked up."

Prez speaks up, "We'll be gettin' outta the way now that you have it under control and I know they're safe."

"Appreciate it," I nod, genuinely. I'm humbled by the support and respect he's shown me, knowing that I'm his daughter's Ol' Man.

He steps over to the bartender, and I feel Princess' body grow stiff, the anger still radiating off of her as I try to eavesdrop.

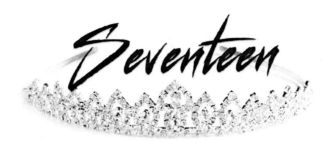

Seventeen

PRINCESS

MY FATHER GLANCES OVER AT THE BARTENDER. "THANKS for the heads-up, Nancy."

She smiles through her discomfort, peering up at him with respect, "Anytime, Prez." She has a towel wrapped around her arm where the bullet grazed her. She's lucky she fell to the floor crying when she was hit; it probably saved her life and also gave her the chance to call my dad.

A gasp escapes me as the knowledge comes to light that she knew who I am and called my dad to tell him I was here. He turns toward me, his eyes soft as he takes me in and begins to speak, but I cut him off.

"How long has she known who I am? Was she calling you every time I was in here?" I fume, with the thought of being watched the entire time. She saw Viking claiming me for heaven's sake. What I do is none of my father's business; he gave up that right many years ago.

"Princess," he starts and I interrupt what I know is about to be some sugarcoated bullshit answer. They always are.

"No. Tell me the truth, damn it. I have a right to know; it's my life."

"I mean, what do you think? You're right down the road from the club, sugar. You're my daughter, and I'm the President of the Oath Keepers. Every bar in the county has had a picture of you and known who you are since you were seventeen years old."

"So...What? You've had people there to spy on me? And what would you have done if I messed up anyhow? You've always been too busy to be a father, so why even care to let them know? Does my privacy mean absolutely nothing to you?"

His eyes become a little glossy as his expression falls flat. "You want the truth, fine. I told them to memorize your face, if you ever showed up, to make sure no one messed with you and if you had any problems ever, to call the club. I paid them well for the favor, but I also threatened to rip their fuckin' guts out if they didn't comply. Like it or not, Princess, you're my kid, and I protect my family."

His words hit my heart like an arrow finding its target. I want to scream and cry, lash out at him with 'why' questions: Why wasn't he there? Why didn't he want us? Why did he hurt everyone? Why weren't we good enough? Why didn't he ever come for us, or actually fucking stay and love us?

I've wondered those things my entire life, but he doesn't deserve my questions, and he hasn't earned my respect to listen to his answers. So, I revert to the only thing that's ever guarded my heart against being completely shattered by him—my words.

Standing a little straighter, I stare down the man standing in front of me. In so many ways we resemble each other. If he had a female version of himself, it would be me; only I don't abandon people that I love.

Many men in this area fear him, never being able to figure out what digs deep, they call him the 'rational' President. He's supposedly the one who thinks everything through and never lets a thing get to him. Well, newsflash, I've had years to perfect just what to say, so it hits home for him. He doesn't get off scot-free ripping our family apart with no repercussions.

I guess I really am like him in one way; I'm the strong one. But I've had to be.

Mimicking him, I shutter any trace of emotion from my face, and then I let the words fly. "I'm with Viking; he's the one who actually protects me. I don't need you; in fact, I've never needed you. My mother stuck around and did everything so you could be a piece of shit sperm donor and go off with your buddies, so please, don't stop now. And while you're gone, do us all a favor and stop breathing."

Brently steps beside us, placing his hand on my arm. "Princess, stop it. You don't know everything."

My father glances sadly at my brother and shakes his head. "No son, don't. Just let it go."

Brently huffs, sending me an irritated glance before letting his hand fall off my arm and moving toward the door.

Glaring spitefully at my father, I practically spit, "I see you've turned him into a good little puppet; nice job, Daddy." I can't help myself; my brother's not the man he used to be, and my father does nothing to steer him from the path he's on. He's going to get Brently fucking killed.

Brently spins suddenly, striding toward me in a rush, bellowing, "Will you just shut the fuck up for once?"

Viking jumps in front of him, stopping Brently mid-stride in his pursuit of me, "Snake, not trying to disrespect you or get involved in your family business and all, but that's my Ol' Lady you're talking crazy to. I won't allow it."

My brother turns toward my father like a good little soldier, waiting for his orders.

"He's right son; she belongs to him. He deals with her, not you."

"She's my fucking sister," Brently argues, and my dad raises his eyebrows. Irritated, my brother meets my hurt gaze. "Fine, you know what? Fuck it. Princess, you wanna act like a spoiled fucking brat? Well, stay the hell away from me."

Viking growls, ready to lay into Brently in my defense, but my brother raises his hands and backs up a few steps, then spins around, storming outside.

Stay away from him? But we've always been there for each other. He was just as screwed up inside as I was growing up. How did I suddenly become the bad guy in all of this? His words slash me inside like razors carving up my flesh. It takes every ounce of pride to stand tall and not start bawling like I want to. Nothing I said was meant to upset my brother.

My father clears his throat, his gaze peering down at my feet as he mumbles, "Sug', when you're ready, we'll talk." He takes a deep breath and turns away.

Passing Viking, my dad pauses long enough to rest his hand on Vike's bicep. I watch intently as he thanks him, expecting my dad to give Viking shit for what just went down, but he doesn't. They shake hands; a mutual respect exchanged and then my father's swiftly out the same door as my brother.

He's gone again. The same as every other time I've seen him in my life. He always takes off, never staying and fighting with me like I wish he would.

"Princess." A raspy grumble comes from the other side of me as Ares angrily follows suit, leaving now that my father's obviously ready and waiting.

I keep quiet as Viking watches the exchange like a hawk.

After a few moments the bar's finally empty, minus the nosey bartender who's stuck cleaning up the huge mess that we've made. Viking strides toward me, pulling me into his embrace. His warmth cocoons me, and I break.

I fucking crumble.

The tears come at me with such a powerful force that my legs give out. I could fall to the floor, and at this moment, I don't care. Everything that just happened with Viking's dad, all the new information and secrets he was hiding from me, from his brothers. After that huge revelation, there was so much hate and violence; I've never seen so much blood before.

The argument with my brother and my father...Brently's words—I can't believe he told me to stay away. I love him; I was protecting us. How can he not see that I'm angry to keep my family from hurting?

Sucking in a sob, my heart and body ache so badly, the only comfort I feel is the heat from this man holding me so desperately, his strength promising me that he'll never let me go. With one arm across my back, keeping me up and against him, he bends a little, tucking his free arm under my butt so he can lift me fully into his embrace.

Complying, I run my hands over his solid chest, wrapping them around his neck and tuck my face against his throat. I'm able to find a sense of peace, being pressed against his heated skin, feeling the pulse beat strongly, reassuring me that he's safe and not leaving me as well.

"Shhh, Cinderella; I've got you, baby," he rumbles quietly, and I feel him start to walk, carrying me to his hotel room.

I try to quiet and slow the tears, but no matter what I think of, my body does what it wants. Viking doesn't complain, though; he just holds me tighter to him.

Once we get inside the room, he carefully lays me in the middle of his bed and then takes his boots off. I turn over to my side, giving him my back and tuck my fists under the pillow I'm lying on. My tears still fall freely; they're just silent now.

The bed dips behind me, and I start to protest that I can't possibly turn it off enough to have sex right now. Viking distracts me so much, but at this moment, my body needs time to process and heal. Before I'm able to form the right words, so I don't hurt him by turning him down, he pulls my back into his body.

His heat engulfs me like a blanket, and I'm shocked to realize that I was so cold and alone when he had laid me down. I felt his warmth on the way over here in his arms, but once I was away from him, I felt nothing.

How can someone break through enough that even when your body is in shock, it still recognizes them?

It feels like we're in bed for hours with daylight fading to dusk. I lie completely silent and still against Viking as my tears escape. He doesn't move once, holding me snuggly against him with his right arm. His head is resting on his left bicep as he softly plays with my hair, gently pulling it off my face as he soundlessly watches me cry. He doesn't have to speak to fix me; he holds me, offering his support and comfort.

For a woman like me, that's all I'll ever need.

The brightness outside slowly disappears until it resembles dimmed lights flooding throughout the room as the sun finally sets and my emotions come to a crashing halt. I've found balance again, but my body's exhausted, feeling as if I haven't slept in days.

The tears stop completely, my tender cheeks starting to dry as my eyes get droopy, and it hits me that for the first time besides my mom, I feel cherished by someone. My heart doesn't weep from being devastated anymore because of my father's actions. Sure it still hurts me a great deal, but I can almost picture it mending back together—piece by jagged piece—as someone else fills up all the little voids with glue, making me whole again. Teaching me to open my heart and love again, not to push them away, but pull them near.

With that blissful thought, my eyes close and I whisper the words that have the power to crush me if they wanted to. They could dismantle me in the end, pull me apart by the seams if used against me. But even with that scary vulnerability exposed, he deserves to hear them, because even if he's my undoing, my heart belongs to him.

"I love you, Vike."

The whisper's soft as it leaves my lips, but with the weight of what those three little words mean to me, it may as well have been a shout as I finally admit it to him out loud.

He doesn't skip a beat, continuing to play with my hair. It's okay, though; I didn't expect him to answer me back. I like to believe inside that he truly cares for me, and right now, that's enough.

Snuggling into the pillow as wonderful sleep starts to overtake my senses, Viking breaks the silence with his deep rasp.

"I know, Cinderella."

Holding my breath, not letting myself succumb yet, I wait for him to tell me it's over, that he can't be tied down, even if I am supposed to be his Ol' Lady.

A few beats pass before he continues, "I've loved you since I found you behind that bar and you looked at me like I was your savior instead of a monster."

He grows quiet, and one last tear slips free as my heart sings with his declaration. Moving my hand to his at my waist, he threads our fingers together and pulls me a little tighter. His lips meet the back of my neck sweetly as I fall into the best sleep of my existence.

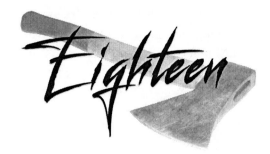

Eighteen

VIKING

The next morning...

A DOOR SLAMS CLOSED, THE NOISE ECHOING THROUGHOUT the small room and disturbing my sleep. Parting my lids, the overly bright sunlight shines in, mocking my splitting headache. Yesterday was a fucking train wreck, to put it mildly.

At some point, Cinderella will hear about me showing up and talking to her father if we end up hanging around the Charter for the barbecue and other get-togethers. Not looking forward to that shit storm.

The bathroom door swings open, my girl coming out with her belongings loaded up in her arms. She heads straight for her purse, dropping everything inside the oversized bag.

"Hey, baby." It comes out sounding extra gruff, my voice a little raw from all the shouting yesterday.

Her fiery gaze meets mine, an eyebrow lifting as I scoot back to sit against the headboard. She ties my wife beater tank at her mid back, so it doesn't swim on her small frame and messily twists her hair up, securing it with a pen from her purse. You'd think with how big the bag is that she'd carry a hair thing in it. Remaining silent, she picks up her cut off shorts from the floor, sliding them on and heads for her flip-flops.

"What're you doing?" I rasp, feeling my forehead wrinkle as my head pounds.

She slips the other shoe on. "Exactly what it looks like. Leaving."

Turning quickly, my feet hit the floor next to my pants. I pull my jeans on, leaving the button unclasped and head over to her so she can't get outside without telling me what's going on.

"You wanna be a little more specific?"

Last night everything seemed to be okay once she calmed down and fell asleep. I know my father scared her, but she's a tough bitch. Besides that, I killed the fucker; she doesn't have to worry about him coming back, ever again. I know my brother will leave her alone, so I don't get why she's upset.

Unless she's pissed at her pops all over again? She's clearly mad about something, as I tower over her, and she glares, probably wishing she could light my ass on fire.

"Nope, sure don't."

"All right, cut the bullshit, Cinderella. The fuck's going on?"

"How should I know? My Ol' Man." She makes quotation marks in the air as she says Ol' Man. "Doesn't tell me anything. I'm just a good little woman, fucking him like I'm supposed to. Guess it makes me the stupid one for thinking we actually had something real."

Pointing my finger close to her face, I warn, "First off, don't you disrespect that title. You'll get a lot of fucking respect you deserve to have from my name being the one attached to it. Second, I don't have any idea what the hell you're talking about. Last night I thought we were straight when you fell asleep. Unless something went down while I was passed out, then shit's still real."

Her gaze lands on the door, and she huffs, "I need to leave," trying to shut me out.

"You can go once we settle this."

"Oh, can I? That's so kind of you. Biker or whoever, you're not my boss and if I want to climb in my car and drive away, then I will." Her stubborn eyes meet mine as she crosses her arms over her chest defiantly.

She's so damn cute, wound up like this.

Smirking, I let out a cocky chuckle, "Baby, if I want you to stay somewhere, you will. You try getting in that car before I say it's okay, and I'll slit your fucking tires."

"You're infuriating. I'll walk if I have to."

"No, you won't. I'll be damned if my woman's walking down that highway. I'll tie you to the bed and eat that pussy until you beg me to let you stay."

"You are pretty talented with that tongue; good to know you don't only use it for lying."

Her retort confuses me. Why would I lie? And about what?

It takes a few seconds until I realize why she's so angry.

"You're pissy 'cause I didn't tell you about my father."

"You're not just some Nomad for the Oath Keepers; you have your own freaking club!"

"You're wrong. That's not my fucking club. I haven't been a Widow Maker in years, and I'll never be again."

Her hands fly up, drastically as she rolls her eyes, "And that name! A widow maker? Yeah, I'd definitely have that on my cut; it sure is something to brag about. I can't believe you haven't told me. Look at the danger you put me in. You kept your past from me, and it almost got me killed. You could have at least told me so I would've been on the lookout."

"You were in the wrong situation, and I'm real sorry about that Princess, but you were never in any danger."

"Look at my arms!" she exclaims, thrusting them out, showing off the ugly bruises my father gave her. "You haven't even seen the cut between my boobs yet. Thank God it wasn't deep!"

My hand goes to her heart, a little rougher than intended and her wide eyes meet mine. "You fuckin' feel that?" Growling angrily, I put pressure on the top of her breast, driving her backward until she hits the wall. "That's your goddamn heartbeat, thumping away. I came for you; I got there as fast as fucking possible, and I killed as many motherfuckers as I had to, to get to you. Don't you tell me that you're hurt unless you're sure you absolutely fucking mean it." And she's wrong; I did see that cut.

Her chest heaves as she gets worked up. "You did save me," she admits quietly, "but you rescued me from your own family that I should have known about."

Sighing deeply, my other hand rakes through my hair, pulling at it in frustration. "I know I fucked up, but you kept your shit from me too." My palm slides over the shirt, stopping at the base of her throat.

"I-I couldn't talk about him to you," she finishes on a whisper, her eyes cresting with tears.

"Yeah, babe, you could. Believe it or not, I do listen to you. I know what it's like to have hate consuming your heart because of fucked-up circumstances."

"He respects you, I could tell. You're angry that I didn't confess, but you already knew who he was to me, didn't you?"

Nodding, I watch as a tear falls down her cheek, then a second, and another, until I can't take them anymore and use my thumbs to wipe her cheeks, wanting her tears to dry. "Shhhh, calm down, everything's all right."

"But it's not." Her lip wiggles as her tears come full force, and I drag her into my arms, holding her tightly to my chest.

"What's going on in that head of yours?"

"You'll hate me," she replies, her voice muffled by my shirt.

"Cinderella, I don't know how you haven't noticed by now, but I'm fucking batshit crazy in love with you. I can't see myself hating you anytime soon, babe."

Her words make me uneasy, but I won't give that away to her. Staring ahead at the beige painted wall, I attempt to swiftly prepare myself mentally for whatever she's going to say.

"I slept with you on purpose."

That's not what I was expecting to leave her mouth, and it almost makes me laugh. "I sorta got that when you rubbed your cum on my lips and flashed me your cunt while you were playing pool."

"God, I'm such a slut."

"Nah, I fucking loved every minute seeing you like that."

"I hooked up with another biker before you."

My hackles rise at the mention of another member. I don't give a shit who the biker is; she belongs to me now.

Princess leans back to look at me, her face red and splotchy from crying, "Me and Bethany had a plan so I could get back at my father."

"Go on."

"I met one of my dad's Prospects before you came along. I used him to upset my father, and I was planning to do the same with you, but you wouldn't let me. Once I was with you, I couldn't even think of anyone else."

"You fuck any of the brothers?" The Prospect was nothing, and I took care of him right away anyhow. No sweat off my back but she better fess up if there was one I don't know about.

"No. You're the only biker I've slept with."

"Good answer."

"It's the truth," she responds, and I close the distance between us.

My palm slides up her shirt, squeezing her full tit as my lips find hers. My other hand eagerly unclasps her shorts button, as my tongue swipes against hers passionately. Within seconds I'm inside her jean shorts, my fingers moving in circles against her clit.

Her dainty hands fly to my jeans, shoving them off my hips as she becomes immersed in sexual need. Her tight fist wraps around my cock eagerly, pumping away with purpose. Tearing my lips from hers, I order hoarsely, "Get on your knees." It's been too long since I've had her. I need to be inside of her now, especially after she gets all mouthy and emotional. She's so fucking beautiful all tearstained and vulnerable, eager to love and please me.

"My knees?" she repeats in a daze.

"Now, Princess."

For once she does exactly what she's told, holding onto my thighs as she drops to the floor directly in front of my cock. Without hesitation, she takes me in as far as she can. It feels incredible, and I'm probably not going to last long like this.

"Deeper, I want to hear you choke on it."

She complies, taking me in several times until she starts to gag. Her reflex and throat massages the sensitive tip making my precum trickle out excitedly.

"Holy fuck, you're gonna make me come so hard like that." Groaning, my mouth hangs open slightly as I watch the fucking goddess in front of me.

Sweat builds on my brow as my nuts begin to tighten in anticipation, yet she continues the pleasurable torture, barely hesitating to catch her breath. Wetness coats her cherry colored swollen lips and chin, making Princess the sexiest bitch I've ever seen before.

She goes even farther on her next pass, causing one of my hands to fly to the wall, steadying my body, so I don't fall over from my knees becoming weak. *She's so damn good.*

"Fuck baby, you wanna swallow my cum, or you want me to fill you up somewhere else?"

She pulls back briefly, staring up at me with desire filling her eyes, continuing to work my cock over with her fist. "I want to please you, Viking. Where do you want it?"

Fuuuuuck. I could shoot all over the place right now with that look and those words.

"I want my cum all over you, especially that pretty face and pink pussy."

Licking her lips, she nods, then bends forward to suck my cock some more. Each pass, she copies my fingers from earlier, swirling her tongue around the head of my cock and sending me one step closer to bliss. My dick begins to throb, and she sits back on her heels, busily pumping me.

The next time I glance down, she's eagerly watching me, her face tilted upwards with her mouth wide open and waiting.

"God, I love that look. I'm going to fuck you so good and hard, everyone will be able to tell I've been beating that pussy up."

A loud growl escapes as cum bursts from my cock, the hot liquid spraying her flushed cheeks and mouth. Halfway through my climax, I spread my seed over her puffy lips and then shove my dick inside. The last of my offering is welcomed by her tongue, as she savors it in her mouth, waiting for me to give her permission to swallow.

"Damn, Cinderella, you make one hell of an Ol' Lady." Muttering, I pull her to her feet and shed my shirt to clean her face for her. "Swallow it."

She nods, softly moaning to herself afterward.

Once she's all taken care of, I walk her over to the bed, having her lie down. My hand shoots between her thighs ready for my turn to play. "Spread those sexy thighs for me, baby."

"I thought you'd need a few minutes?" She gasps as I find her clit again.

"Fuck that, now open up so I can watch as I finger fuck that sugary cunt."

With each pump of my fingers her core clenches, trying to pull them in further, her pussy creaming around my knuckles.

"I swear if I can eat you out every day of my life, I'll die a happy man."

"The stuff you say to me, it's crazy. I'm not used to anyone talking to me like that, and it makes me want you constantly."

Pulling my fingers free, I use the wetness to insert them in her ass while my tongue hungrily swipes up any leftover juice in her slit. Her honey hits my taste buds, and my cock instantly stiffens, ready for more.

"Ahhh!" she calls out, her body tightening up on me.

Keeping up my assault, I run my tongue from her pink folds, spreading her wetness down her taint, eventually pushing cream and saliva into her back entrance. She goes wild, her body squirming and as soon as it's lubed enough, my digits go right back in, working her over as my lips slurp her slit and suck on her clit.

I don't stop until she screams, coming all over my chin and lips. Like the greedy bastard that I am, I lick up every last drop my tongue can find then flip her onto her stomach.

"Oh my god!" she mumbles into the bedspread.

Grabbing her hips, I prop her ass in the air, rubbing my tip all over her cunt until she starts gyrating, attempting to get my dick to slip in farther. After a few moments of teasing her, I line myself up with her asshole. She stills just like I figured she would, sliding my hand around her hip and between her thighs, I find her core. Shoving three fingers in deep, I plant my cock in her ass at the same time.

"Please not like the first night," she whispers, but even low, I can still hear the tears in her voice.

I loved the first night.

Stilling, I take it down a notch and start kissing up her back, pausing next to her ear to murmur, "I don't think you realize how much control you really have, Cinderella. I loved the first night, but I love you so much more. Tell me what you want, baby; tonight is all yours."

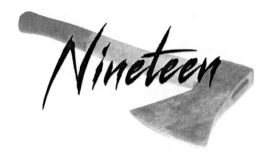

Nineteen

VIKING

Saturday…

"ALL RIGHT, TAKE A SEAT."

Nancy, the bartender, was nice enough to let us borrow the bar for an hour before she has to come in and do her daily setup. Scot offered to take her to lunch on my dime, and she excitedly obliged. I had no clue that she's the one who owns the place. I've gained a lot of respect for that lady since I've been here.

"Stacy, the chick that helps out at night here, dropped off some muffins and shit that she baked. Help yourselves, just remember it next time you leave her a tip."

Everyone eagerly grabs three or four different muffins, munching away, content. I'm glad they have something to help smooth over what I'm about to discuss with them. "Odin, grab a few pitchers of water and some plastic cups."

"Seriously?" He cocks his eyebrow at me like I'm fucking nuts.

"You want a real shot at being in the MC? You want to go to the barbecue later?"

"You're really going to boss me around and shit now, huh?" He so much like me, it's unreal. Princess told me last night that she's going to go bald in a few years having two of us broody assholes around. I just laughed and asked if she'd bake us a cherry pie.

Breathing deeply, I attempt to tune in the patience that Princess has been helping me with the past few days. "We talked about this yesterday. I'm not fucking Jekyll, and things will be changing, for you, me, for all of us." I glance around at the brothers surrounding our makeshift church table. We pushed a few small square tables together, and I'm at the head. Blaze and Torch are at my sides.

Eventually, Odin will take his spot beside me. He's my brother, and once I'm able to teach him about true brotherhood like I've learned with the Nomads, he'll become my Vice President. Right now, though, he's not allowed at the table. My father treated him like a regular member, so he was pissed to hear he'd been essentially demoted. What he doesn't understand is that he should have been treated like a kid and never even saw the table in the first place.

Smokey's at the end along with Bronx, he's the new kid I had gut checked outside the bar. I think with Ares and Exterminator getting hits in after me, the kid was traumatized enough to welcome some change. Butters and Charlie would be down there as well, but they're dead. Can't say that I care either. If anything, I'm glad because they were fucking scum, just like Jekyll.

Rapping my knuckles on the table, everyone's gazes fall to me.

"First off, let's make one thing clear, I'm not Jekyll," I repeat myself from earlier, but this time to the brothers. "Got it?"

I'm met with 'ayes' all around, and surprisingly they seem excited about that aspect. It shouldn't be a surprise I suppose with the miserable tyrant my father was. Odin comes back setting everything in the middle of us, then sits back at the bar as I instructed him to when we first arrived. Glad he's paying attention.

"What's the deal with the clubhouse?" We used to have a rundown building in the middle of nowhere that the MC drank and discussed business. It wasn't anything compared to the Compounds I've grown used to in the past few years.

Torch speaks up, "We use it as a chop shop now when we're home."

"Fuck. You'll get popped and do years in the pen."

Blaze huffs, his eye still a deep purple from my fist finding out that he touched my woman's hair. "A few of us tried to say that, but you know when Jekyll got an idea, it was no stopping him."

"Who ran it?"

"That was O's contribution."

I swear to Christ my eyes bug the fuck out of my head. "My brother?"

Everyone nods, not meeting my eyes.

One, two, three, fifty, a hundred, think of Princess, don't break anyone's face, and just breathe.

"No more. It ends now. Blaze, find someone you can hire to gut it out and fucking burn everything."

He chuckles. "And how do we pay for this?"

"Who usually handles the books?"

"Charlie, but there wasn't much of anything to be counted. The money we're using now to be here was from our recent drug sale on the way over here."

"Fuck. Okay, was it a decent pay out?"

"We each got a five hundred dollar cut."

"You fuckin' with me right now?" How can you do a drug run and only cut your men five bills for serious possible jail time? That doesn't build loyalty; it builds rats and sellouts when they're presented with more paper.

"Odin, call my woman and ask her to stop by with five g's."

Everyone stares at me, shocked and silent.

"That's bad business and bad dealing. I'll give you each a grand. Don't go screw it off on blow. Save a few hundred for shit you need to take care of. From now on, we'll be voting on club business. Temporarily, I'd like for Blaze to sit as my VP until Odin is ready. It could be two years or ten, who knows. Torch deserves the Death Dealer patch. Smokey if you're still decent with numbers, you can start up the books and trade your patch for Treasurer? We need a decent cash counter, and I'll be paying close attention to all of it. Bronx, we'll give it a little time and see if you get something other than member. Everyone agree to that?"

They all reply 'aye' except Blaze.

"I'll lose my Death Dealer patch? But what happens when Odin is ready to take over as VP?"

"You can have your Death Dealer patch back, or we can vote on a different one if that's what you want."

"Okay, I vote 'aye.'"

"We'll be recruiting, but not many. I want us to get our feet on the ground and adapt before growing too much. There were at least nine more when I was at home. Where is everyone?"

Blaze takes a drink of water and replies since everyone else stays quiet. "Dead."

"Fuck." I shake my head, nine dead, plus the two from the other day, eleven members. That's horrible. "I'm meeting with the Prez from the Oath Keepers Charter here later. I want to see if he'll offer us a patch over and a few potential business partners."

"What the fuck? South Carolina already has an OK Chapter," Smokey declares. Being an older member of the MC, I'm expecting a lot of fight from him.

"I know, which will give you three options. One, if this patch over happens, you will be given the option to leave. Two, you will have a place in the South Carolina Charter or pretty much any other location. I actually know the Prez down there, and he's a good man. Three, I will step up and run my family's club, but my Ol' Lady's life is here. As it turns out, my life is going to be here with her, so my chapter will be built in this area, and you will be offered a place in it. I won't have the Compound in this exact place, but close. There's many clubs in Austin, and they have a good relationship with the Oath Keepers."

Torch sighs, "Well fuck, some of us can't afford to just pick up and move our shit; I have a little girl to think about."

"Actually, since there's only a few of you, yes, you can. I'll make sure you get here."

"And where will we sleep, what will we eat? I wasn't really getting by, and that's with anything from the club and a part-time job."

"I'll look into purchasing land and start a build on a basic clubhouse. Singles can have a room there, but you'll have to keep it clean. Anyone with a family or kids, we'll get it figured out."

Bronx interrupts, "I'm in; I don't need to go back at all."

Smokey takes a drag of his cigarette, rasping, "And where will this money come from exactly?"

"For the past five years, I've bought a new bike, food and stayed in occasional cheap-ass motels. I don't have a lot, but I have enough to put a chunk down to get started. I'm gonna ask my Ol' Lady's father for input and help. The Oath Keepers are different from the Widows; they make some pretty damn good cheddar. It'll be tough at first; I'm not going to lie, but I believe in a few years, shit will be really good."

Blaze sits up. "I'm in."

Smokey releases the toxic smoke from his lungs as he talks, "Why would you do this for us? You took off when Jekyll fucked you up and sent you on a stripe, never coming back."

"Because that stripe saved my life, they took me in and showed me what brotherhood is. After experiencing it, I know everyone deserves it."

He nods.

"That's another thing, the Nomads. You saw them the other day, except for one. If this works, I'm inviting them to join the Chapter and just saying this up front; they'll be full members and offered officer patches."

A few grumble and it takes everything inside to tamper down my temper.

"That's fine, you feel that way, but one saved my ass the other morning from a fucking lion. How many of you know of a brother that has your six like that? I've never met a more loyal, fearless group of men before. Do not underestimate any of them, ever."

Bronx rolls his eyes, but he'll learn when Ex beats the hell out of him for that shit.

"We're all invited to their barbecue later, and I think it would be in our best interest to go and make friends. The Prez offered to let you stay in their guest rooms if needed. I know a few of the members from handling a job with them and stopping through on runs. You can relax around them and have a beer; they won't try to kill you in your sleep. You'll get a good look at the Oath Keeper life." They stay silent, so I figure it's time to call it to an end. "Anyone have anything to add?"

Torch nods. "We're in."

Smokey follows. "Yup, me too. Been wanting to get outta SC for years, just wasn't able to."

"Welcome to Texas, brothers."

Rapping my knuckles against the table to note the end of the first church I've conducted, I'm wearing a smile when it's over.

PRINCESS

HAVING ODIN ASK ME FOR FIVE GRAND IN CASH, HAD ME A little skeptical, but being Viking's brother, I figure I should give him a chance. I went to drop it off, and he climbed in the car asking if he could come back to the apartment with me instead of staying with his older brother. I ended up taking him with me grocery shopping to get a few things for the barbecue tonight, and we left with two hundred dollars' worth of food.

To see him so excited over having that much food, kind of broke my heart a little. He shared with me that he never really went grocery shopping like that before. I guess he only visited the store for basic things that he could stretch out to last him a long time, like peanut butter and bread. Once I heard that I encouraged him to throw whatever he wanted into the cart. Viking had stuffed five hundred dollars in my purse a few days prior, making up for all the food I was cooking them, but I didn't want to use it. If it's for his brother, though, then I don't mind.

Never in a million years would I have thought that he's only fifteen. I knew he was young, but he's weathered for his age, and that makes me so sad for him. My father sucked, but Odin grew up without love, like my Viking. And shit can he eat; my God, he clears his plate and eats anything else I load it with.

Viking had brought his stuff over to my apartment so Odin would be able to sleep on the couch and not be left alone. He's worried that Odin may get pissed about something and just leave without letting us know. I was a little nervous about them being in my space twenty-four hours a day, but I love it. I didn't realize before that I was so lonely all the time when Bethany wasn't around.

I've loved having Viking talk to me a lot over the past few days and ask my opinions on everything. We've been trying to come up with a plan that would make us both happy. He's so distraught about the fact that he has to leave the Nomads. They're his family, people who get him and don't judge. Now he's being thrown into something he never wanted in the first place.

When he told me that he was going to stay here and be home a lot, I almost did cartwheels I was so excited about it. He wants to find a small two-bedroom house for us to rent, so he can give Odin some stability here, and I can't blame him. After meeting Jekyll, Odin's going to need every ounce of help and structure he can get. I'm young and know jack about teenagers, but I swore to Vike that I'd do my best and support him as much as I can.

My father and I haven't spoken since our blowup, but I've been thinking a ton about what all he and my brother were saying. I was so upset that I didn't pay much attention at the time it was all happening. Now, though, I'm growing curious.

We stopped by my mom's yesterday, but again, she wasn't home. I wanted her to get to meet Viking. It was the same way as before with my dad and brother's Softails parked there and the truck missing. I'm starting to freak out; it's been two months since I've physically seen her and about a month that we've spoken to each other and not just in random messages.

Viking told me that he was meeting with Prez today but that he wasn't going to the barbecue. I'm relieved I won't have to worry about a confrontation, but I was kind of hoping to at least ask if he's seen her. I just want to make sure she's okay. In her last message she sounded like she was desperate to see me, but now it's almost as if she's avoiding me.

There's nothing I can do, besides keep trying and ask my dad or Brently if I see them.

Once my mom's famous Italian pasta salad is complete, I paint on some light makeup and dig through my closet. I need to find something that's fit for a biker bitch to wear but also says I'm the Ol' Lady to a President of an outlaw MC. One benefit of having my mom as the Prez' Ol' Lady, she knew how to dress.

Settling on some thigh-high black leather boots with four-inch heels, I pair them with a cherry red leather miniskirt and my black Harley tank top. Finishing the look, I use a blood red lipstick that's smudge proof and tie my hair in a high ponytail. We'll be riding his bike, and I'm not showing up with my hair looking like a hot mess.

His stack of bandanas that I washed sits folded perfectly on the counter spurring my idea further. I pick out the nicest looking black one, fold it a few times and wrap it over my hair. It reminds me of those workout headbands you use to hold your bangs back; only this one is much more badass.

"Odin, do you drive? I can't carry the pasta salad on Viking's bike; the bowl's too large." He doesn't respond, so I turn around to make sure I'm not waking him up or something.

I'm met with large eyes and his mouth slightly hanging open.

"Odin?"

"You're wearing that?"

"Umm, yes. Is it not good?"

"Do you want my brother to kill someone tonight? 'Cause if you wear that outfit, that's what will end up happening."

"Whatever, it'll be fine." I laugh and roll my eyes. "Do you drive?"

"I can."

"Perfect, I need you to follow us with the pasta salad."

"Cool."

"Thanks."

He nods and the front door opens; Viking's finally back.

"Hey! How'd it go?"

Viking takes his boots off next to the door like I previously asked him to and started peeling the few chunky rings he wears and such off, not glancing up yet. "Fucking perfect. We did a little tweaking and shit, but overall it's going to work out. We're going to settle about twenty miles out at an old pig farm. Best fuckin' part is, your dad's gonna work with me on making him payments so I can start the build on the club right away."

"That's amazing news!"

"Yeah, I'm so fucking stoked." He glances up and goes silent, just standing and staring.

"Vike?" I raise my eyebrow.

"I'm going to kill someone tonight," he finally answers, and Odin pops in.

"Told you."

"Should I change?" I don't want to and wouldn't any other time, but this is the first time he's riding with his club to meet another MC. I want it to be his night.

"Fuck no; you're the sexiest woman I've ever seen."

"Hell, yeah," Odin comments and Viking growls.

"Shut up." His eyes glaze over looking at me again. "I need to shower, or we'll never fucking leave." He storms off, and I do a little dance inside, knowing that I've made him proud.

Twenty

PRINCESS

THE RIDE OVER ISN'T BAD AT ALL; IF ANYTHING, I'M REALLY starting to enjoy Viking sharing this with me. I know he loves the wind and road when he's on his Harley, and that means something special to me because I love him. Pulling into the Compound is a little nerve racking. I was made to stay away basically my entire life and now to be invited, is just surreal.

The night passes in a blur; Viking's introduced me to so many people. Blaze and Torch actually smiled at me; I thought their faces were going to crack or something. I think my favorites are still the Nomads. I got used to their banter and rough exteriors. Plus, I know they truly have Viking's back, and that's important to me.

God, I wanted so badly to rip Nightmare a new one, but know that I can't. He's Bethany's baby's dad, and she needs to fight that battle when she's ready. I'll always support her decisions even if I don't agree with them.

However, I was a little taken back though when he was talking to me like nothing was different. Nightmare has to know I'd be pissed at him on my best friend's behalf. Once he said hello and started telling me that Viking had to patch him up on their run, I just walked off in the middle of him talking. He's Vike's brother, not mine.

I met the Oath Keepers Ol' Ladies, which was interesting. They all have big personalities, and you can tell they love their own type of sisterhood that they've formed. I was nervous, but Ares and 2 Piece's Ol' Lady, Avery, walked right up to me and started talking like she'd known me for years. I couldn't believe it when she told me she had two Ol' Men; I wasn't sure if I should feel bad for the woman or congratulate her.

There was also a rumor floating around that my dad may pass the gavel to his VP, who happens to be Ares. I was freaking shocked, and now I do want to speak to him. The only part of the night I'd take back if I could, would be catching Odin with an Oath Keeper's little sister bent over the trunk of my damn car.

Pretty sure that it was Spin's little sister too, but I'm pretending like I didn't see a thing. Maybe Oath Keeper women will end up falling for Widow Maker men, who knows. I did warn Vike, though, and he had a 'talk' with Odin. The kid was mortified, but it was hilarious and the least he deserved. I don't think he understands what kind of hell he can stir up for himself messing with a biker's little sister.

After this brief time, I'm starting to see why my mom loved this life in so many ways; I can understand why it made her so happy with my father. Bikers don't just love you; they obsess over you. With that fierce love, comes a protection like no other, willing to kill for their women at a drop of a hat. Getting together didn't make me feel uncomfortable or out of place like I imagined it would. I felt like I was finally home and surrounded by family. I was hugged and welcomed, complimented on my food and asked to come back.

If this is club life, no wonder my father loves it, because I do too.

VIKING

The following day...

YESTERDAY I MET WITH PREZ AND MY NOMAD BROTHERS. I wanted everyone's opinion on my ideas to merge the club over. They were a little hesitant at first, but once I explained all of it out in detail, they were much more open then I'd expected.

There was a vote, and I was named the new President of a hybrid Charter. Prez said he'd contact the other Charters to inform them of us and the decision. After being a part of the Oath Keepers, I know what types of men are in the MC, and I'm pretty honored to be a President affiliated with them.

Ares was in that meeting and surprisingly he approved of the plans.

I also found out about the run to Mexico we pulled since Exterminator was there. He said that he let the cop know about the maid and then hours later some mafia guys in suits showed up and took her. According to Ex, the Russians are on a massive manhunt for one of their sisters that were taken. The cop asked to use us in the future, and Ex agreed as long as there are no exotic animals involved.

I'm hoping with the time it'll take to build our Compound and get everything set up that my Nomad brothers will trade their wanderer patch for one that says Texas. I can't think of any better men to have in my club.

Nightmare showed up to the meeting. He thought Ex was bull-shitting him about everything that was going down and he needed proof. It was pretty fuckin' hard to watch him walk in using a cane. He claimed that once it's healed, he won't need it, but I was the one who saw the gash first, and I'd be surprised if he ever walked without it again. He was at the party but stayed sitting, so I had missed it.

Scot came too. He asked the brothers to approve his request to hand in his Nomad patch. He's not planning on leaving Nancy anytime soon and asked to be a part of my hybrid crew. I was honored.

Being surrounded by my brothers made me realize just how lucky Odin is going to be. He not only has Princess fawning all over him, feeding him too much, but he's going to learn the true meaning of brotherhood and loyalty.

Before I left yesterday, Prez pulled me to the side and requested I bring my woman to her mom's house. I tried to let him know I wasn't getting in the middle of their relationship shit, but he reassured me it's because her mom needs to see her and that he wouldn't cause trouble.

We're headed to her house now, and I'm a tad bit nervous how she'll take the news of Princess and me. Of course, I won't care if she's not welcoming, but I want this part of our relationship to be somewhat easy on my woman. She's already dealt with way too much when it comes to me and our family drama.

"You straight, Cinderella?" I check as we dismount off my bike.

I've been asking her randomly ever since I found out how bad her anxiety can get. I never want to see my Ol' Lady shut down like she did when my father had her. She admitted that it happened the first night we saw each other also with the attack. I guess she felt strong with me there beside her, but that once she was away from me her tears and shakes set in for a few hours.

"I'll be fine; I'm just happy we're finally getting a chance to visit, and you're meeting her."

"Me too, baby." I place a swift peck on her lips and follow her up the pathway.

We climb the stairs to the porch, and she stops mid-stride. "The door's painted," she mutters softly.

"Yeah?"

Clearing her throat after a moment, she knocks on the front door. Pulling her hand to her chest, she rubs her knuckles with her fingertips. I don't know what's up with the sudden weirdness, but somethings gotten to her.

Her brother opens the door, stepping out of the way for us to enter. "P." He greets her, then turns to me, "Viking." He nods and I return it.

Prez comes into the dainty living room looking exhausted; he has dark bags under his eyes, and he's dressed in plain clothes. You'd never guess that he's the President of an MC, seeing him like this.

The couch has sheets, and a pillow pushed carelessly to the side and a half eaten grilled cheese sits on the coffee table in front of it. Princess notices and becomes annoyed, "Geez Brent, you need to clean up your crap. You're too old to be making Mom do it. Did you move back in?"

He huffs, "No, of course not. That's Dad's, not mine."

Prez approaches us, "Heya, sug', thanks for coming," he says to Princess then turns to me shaking my hand, "Brother."

"Brother," I respond, paying him the same respect.

"Mom?" Princess calls but gets no answer.

Prez cuts straight in, "We need to talk about your momma."

"What's wrong with her? What did you do this time?"

PRINCESS

FURIOUS AT THE MESS MY DAD'S LEFT MY MOTHER TO DEAL with, I question him, ready for him to admit that he's staying here to have her wait on him like he sometimes does. He'll walk through the door after being gone months, and you'd swear he was a long lost king or something with how my mom treats him.

His hand tangles in his overly long sandy hair as his head drops, his eyes on the floor instead of meeting my irate gaze. He opens his mouth to say something, but then a huge crash comes from my mom's bedroom.

"I've got it, Dad," Brently jumps, but my dad rushes in front of him.

"No son! Not unless it's absolutely necessary."

"It is, talk to Princess so that she can stop this bullshit."

"Excuse me?" I gape at him. Who the fuck does he think he is, suddenly being a dick to me all the time. I've barely walked in the freaking house.

A moan comes next from my mom's room, and I quickly skirt around the table, beelining for the bedroom door.

"Wait!" My father shouts, but I ignore him, throwing the door open.

"Mom?" It takes a second to see a table knocked over with stuff spilled everywhere. I find her on the floor, crumpled in a small, frail ball, a small amount of throw up beside her.

"Shit! Mom! Are you okay?" Rushing over to her side, I start to help turn her over when I'm stopped by a firm hand. My head shoots up, finding my father's stern gaze.

"Don't move her like that," he orders and I yank my shoulder out of his grip.

"Get off me; I'll take care of her. I always make sure she's okay."

"I know," my dad croaks as tears start to fall down his cheeks. I've only seen him cry one time in my life, and I thought I had hallucinated it all. "I know you do sweetheart, and I'll owe you for the rest of my life for taking such good care of the woman I love."

"What are you talking about?" I'm so fucking confused. What is going on?

His shoulders shake as sobs begin to take over. Brently comes in to help Mom to bed, and Dad just bawls, so much to the point that I start crying. It's so fucking scary to see the man that you've always known to be unreadable and hard, crack before your eyes.

"Dad, talk to me please, what the hell's happening?" I glance at my mom, clearly on a ton of medication looking the weakest I've ever seen her. Brently fixes her pillow and softly wipes off her cheek with a baby wipe.

That's when I notice it...I see a big piece of her hair's missing, and I know exactly why she's been so absent. She's been hiding it from me. With a hoarse cry I turn to my father, my watery eyes overfilling and blurry to where I can only make out his shape. "God no! Please, no, please, please, please tell me she's okay. I have to be wrong; this can't be happening."

"I'm so sorry, sugar."

"No!" A guttural bark leaves my mouth, shaking my head.

"I'm sorry," he repeats, and I get so irate inside.

"Fuck. You! Get out of my mom's house, you piece of shit! Get the fuck out, all of you; she was fine when I was here with her!"

Viking forcibly wraps his huge arms around my body, pulling me up off the floor and carrying me out into the living room while I scream at everyone, blaming them for this tragedy. It's not an easy feat for him as I kick and scream, weeping that my mother is in that bed dying, and he's taking me away from her.

"Shhh, Cinderella," he repeats softly into my hair, tightly cocooning me in his warmth until I'm too sad and worn out to fight any longer. The one person that's been there for me my whole life, my constant, is lying in that bed, struggling for her life. And no one told me before it was so late.

Once I'm silently crying, he sits on the small sofa with me in his lap, sweetly playing with my hair like he did the night he saw me freak out. The thought of my mother looking so frail is terrifying. She's always been so stubborn and strong, her only weakness being my father, and now this.

My dad and brother eventually come out of her room and sit on the couch, both with their own tears coating their scruffy faces.

Viking, ever my strength, starts talking. "I can understand why this wasn't said over the phone, but Princess should have been notified sooner. How can she have time to make peace?" he directs at my father.

"None of us have. My wife's been sick for a long time, but she's kept it from her family. She's always been like that, though when something's been wrong with her. I came over one night and found her passed out on the kitchen floor. The doctor said by her body and tests that she had probably been there for longer than twenty-four hours. We don't know if she was out the whole time or not, but he said her body shut down to throw it in protection mode and that if it would have been longer, then she would have most likely passed. That was about two months ago."

"When you started answering her phone?" I ask quietly.

His defeated gaze meets mine. "Yeah. Then it progressed so rapidly. She told me she could beat it, and she didn't want either of you to know unless it looked like she wouldn't make it. The minute she had an ounce of energy, I'd call you and have her leave you messages. This last week's been the worse; she was in the hospital for most of it. I was hoping she would bounce back, but at this point, there's no telling. It's up to her body and the medicine to work together and fight back."

"She can't have surgery or something to get it removed?"

"Not until she makes it through this round of medicine. Believe me, honey, I'm on them, calling her doctors daily, leaving messages about her having surgery. I even tried to bribe the doctors with the money I have set aside for you guys. Ares went as far as threatening to kill one surgeon. I had to talk him down and pay the man off. He wasn't even the right kind of doctor had he gotten the guy to agree eventually. It's been one giant clusterfuck."

"So what do we do then?" Sitting up, Viking's big hands wipe away my tears, always taking care of me.

"We wait and see, but in the meantime, you tell her you love her as much as you can."

"I can do that." I nod. "Does she have a nurse that helps out?"

"Yeah, but she doesn't like anyone seein' her like that. You know how beautiful your momma's always been and stubborn. She doesn't like help when she's sick."

"So what happened in there earlier?"

"If she wakes and is going to be sick, she tries to make it on her own instead of saving her energy like we beg her to do."

"I don't even know what to say."

"You don't have to say anything, sug'."

"I'm surprised you're here so much. Is that why there's rumors about Ares being President?"

He nods. "Yeah, I uh, I told him that I've had to stay away from her long enough, I'm not wasting anymore time."

"You could have been here the entire time; you made her fall apart every time you left. I was the one behind with her, helping her pull it back together. You didn't just do it once either; you did it over and over, and she'd be a mess for days, weeks; hell, sometimes for a full month. But now that she's sick, you want to play hero?" I can't stop the words tumbling out as my emotions spiral.

"I know. I tried to stay away, but I loved her too much. I'd stay gone for as long as I could handle, but I always came home eventually."

"Ha. That sounds pathetic; really you had to stay away? Really? We were your family, your wife, and children. We wanted you!"

"I know it, but I couldn't fucking help it!" His voice increases as his eyes start to dry. "I had to stay away. It wasn't my choice; it was for your safety after I received threat-amongst threat against you all. I had to keep you safe. I knew if you hated me, you'd stay away from me and no one could get to you. I get it; I fucked up your life. I know that, and I live with it every fucking day. You don't think I wanted my life?" He points toward my mom's room, "That woman has owned me since I first laid eyes on her!"

"So what's different now that you can come right back into everything?"

"My son is grown and has brothers that will help him if needed. My beautiful daughter is the Ol' Lady of the President of an MC club, who'd blow up half the fucking country to find her. You're both safe, *finally*. If they come for me, well they can have my life. I only care about my wife being alive and healthy and my children."

"Look, Dad, I want to believe you, I really do. I promise to try, okay?" My mother's sick, she wouldn't want her family fighting like this. If I have to bite the bullet and back off, I will.

This whole time, I was trying to protect her, and I'd even go to extreme lengths to do it, just like my father did. I only wish that I'd known that I was protecting her against the wrong thing. I was too busy hating my father when I should have been loving my mother.

Thank God, I've found a love so strong with Viking because I'm going to need the extra backbone and support when I help my mom kick cancer's ass. She's a stubborn Ol' Lady who leads the pack; in my heart, I know she'll win, and she'll finally get her man.

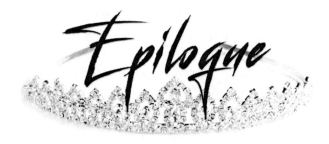

Epilogue

PRINCESS

One year later...

"GET MORE PLATES!" I YELL TOWARD THE MAIN ROOM AT Odin.

"Yes, ma'am," he calls back, using his sweet manners he's developed over the past year. Viking's been ruthless about Odin growing into a decent man and not like Jekyll. When we finally have kids of our own, they're going to be little angels or risk getting 'the talk' from Viking all the time. I love his voice, but he can drone on to teenagers, and they hate that shit.

Odin comes in carrying a stack, stopping at the end of the table, "Where do you need them?"

"That's fine; you can stack them there and then when everyone comes in they can fix their plates and either sit with us or wherever. I don't want any pressure since they've been good at letting me take over the clubhouse for the past few days."

"They should be in here helping; you did cook enough food for an army."

Shrugging, I smile kindly at him, "No big deal, it's Thanksgiving, and this is how it should be for everyone."

Nancy passes in the hallway, waving when she notices me. She wanted to help out, and I gladly obliged. She's made all the desserts for tonight, and they look so delicious. I can't wait to try out her key lime pie.

"Are we still stopping by Mom's later?" Odin started calling my mother "Mom" about six months ago. I couldn't be any happier about it either.

"Yep, you're still coming right?"

"Of course."

"Okay, just checking, I didn't know if you had plans with Mercy or not."

He's been dating Spin's younger sister off and on for a while now. The only way Spin agreed not to kill him was because Viking promised to take care of it himself if Odin got her pregnant. Mercy's about to turn sixteen and full of mischief. But she's close to Odin's age, which I love because he spends too much time around adults.

"Nope, I'll be there," he replies as Viking carries food in from the kitchen.

"Damn, Cinderella; this shit smells so fuckin' good."

"I know, I'm starving. Is my dad here yet?"

"Yeah, he's drinking a whiskey."

"Shit, again?"

He nods.

"Try to keep him distracted or pour some water in it, something. I don't want him blurring today out. We need to be happy and eat some good food."

"I got it, baby, don't worry. Ares is here, too. You know that's practically his father too. He'll keep him talking."

"All right, God, I really don't know what I'd do without you. I love you so much, Vike. More every day."

"You want some D, huh?"

Laughing, I shake my head "I say love, and you automatically think of your cock?"

"Hey, I'm pretty sure that's why you fell for me," he says aloud, then mouths out 'cunt crazy.' He's been teasing me about it more here lately with Avery popping up pregnant. He's lost it if he thinks it's happening with me anytime soon. I'm too selfish, I want him all alone, at least for a few more years. I don't think I'll ever get my fill of him.

As we gather around the massive tables we rented for this dinner; I can't help but think about how lucky I am. I'm surrounded by friends and family I adore and sitting next to the man of my dreams that I never even knew I wanted.

Oh, and then there's the billiards table Viking brought home on our anniversary. That alone is enough reason to love him forever.

VIKING

"HEY, PREZ?"

"What?" Ares and I answer at the same time, then chuckle. We've grown used to it now since we're together a lot.

It's one of his guys; Shooter comes closer to speak to Ares about a shipment of weapons, and I turn away.

"Brother, you can stay," Ares mumbles.

"Nah, I'm good, I need to go be sociable." Chuckling, I head through the club, just taking it all in.

Every day, I walk through with a cup of coffee, first thing and check everything over. It's surreal knowing that I built this club. We've grown a lot too. It's still Smokey, Blaze, Torch, and Bronx, but now we also have Scot, Nightmare, Saint, Sinner. And our newest brother, Chaos.

When the club was built, I asked all the Nomads to join us, but they weren't ready to trade in their patch yet, which is fine. They stop in from time to time and catch up. I've made it very clear that they'll always have a place here waiting for them.

Growing up, I thought I'd never have anything, and now I feel like I've got it all. I have strong, loyal brothers at my table, and Odin is thriving. He actually walks around smiling sometimes. My club is running successfully, finally making some decent money and I've got the best fuckin' bitch a biker could ever wish for.

ODIN

AFTER WE EAT, I HELP PRINCESS CLEAR OFF THE TABLE. I'VE learned that if I help her out, then she'll let me use her car or take me with her when she grocery shops. I've gained twenty pounds since I came to live with her and my brother. At this rate, I'll be bigger than him in no time.

Making an excuse to be back, I grab my favorite club whore's wrist, tugging her along behind me. They don't realize I'm about to be seventeen, or they do and just don't care. We get to the bathroom, and I pull her into the largest stall, pushing lightly on her shoulders.

Sinking to her knees eagerly, she opens my pants enough to free my stiff cock. The food was good, but once the turkey settled, all I could think of was how damn horny I'd become.

Immediately, she takes my length in her warm, wet mouth as far as she can go, her eyes widening as I get closer to her throat. The club whores like to take turns with me to see if one can make me say anything. I don't moan or talk; I'm there to get off not hear my voice.

She starts in on my favorite move. I like to call it the 'Triple Whammy.' She's the only one who does it, gripping my cock tightly she twists her palm over the base, at the same time she uses her nails to scratch lightly over my sack and continue to suck on my cock. All at once.

Within minutes she has me exploding, pumping my cum down her throat in pure ecstasy.

Once we're cleaned up, I offer to find her later and finger fuck her if she wants. She's a club whore, so of course she agrees.

Mercy sends me a text, freaking out because I haven't messaged her all day, but I ignore it. Instead, I grab the flowers off my dresser that I bought earlier when I went to pick up ice for the club. Tossing them in the passenger seat of Princess' car, I head over to Mom's; thinking on the way about Mercy breaking up with me a few weeks ago. I haven't told anyone about it yet.

Last year when Mom got so sick, we were over there pretty much every day with Princess. When Mom was having a good day, I'd sit in her room with her, and she'd tell me a bunch of crazy stories about everything. Then when she'd had a bad day, I'd hold her hand and tell her how important she was to us all.

My brother thinks I've made changes because of him, but it was really for her. I didn't want mom to know my cold side, especially when she filled my heart with so much love.

Picking up the flowers, I remove the outer plastic wrap, throwing it on the floorboard. She was in luck at the store; I found her favorites, a big bundle of Gerbera daisies. I try not to slam the door as I climb out, but the wind catches it, making the noise echo around me.

Princess still meets me with a friendly wave regardless. She thinks she's like her father, which she is, but she's also filled to the brim with warmth from her mother.

My brother lets her go long enough for her to wrap me in a hug and smell the flowers. Tilting her head up, her eyes shiny with tears, she smiles softly and whispers, "She will love them, Odin. You make me so proud to have you in my life."

When she releases me, I bend; kneeling at Mom's grave to whisper how much I miss her, but also to thank her for leaving me with someone who loves me.

Note:

This may not be the ending you were hoping for. It wasn't for me either. I cried the entire time I wrote it, even during the sexy times because I could feel where this story was taking me, and I was fighting it. I'm still crying as I write this. I feel like I'm betraying Prez by not giving him his happily ever after, but through life comes hardships. While this is fiction, I want to bring you pieces of realistic hardships people face as well.

I want you to smile at funny parts, get excited during a sex scene, anxious when there's suspense and most of all I want you to cry if a part makes you sad enough to. If any of that happens, then I did my job by making you *feel*. If you were able to experience even a fraction of what I felt when writing it, then thank you. That's the best compliment I can receive.

XOXO
Sapphire

Acknowledgements

My husband - I love you more with each book I write. You drive me crazy some days, but you make up for it by being hot.

My boys - You are my whole world. I love you both. This never changes, and you better not be reading these books until you're thirty and tell yourself your momma did not write them!

The lovely beta readers - Abbey Neil-Clark, Sarah Rogers, Lindsay Lupher, Wendi Stacilaucki-Hunsicker, Patti Novia West, and Jamey Weber. Thank you for all the love you've shown me. You've all helped me grow tremendously in my writing, and I'm forever grateful. I had so much fun reading through your comments and suggestions on this book; I'm so happy you love it!

Photographer and Model Darren Birks – Thank you for selling me such a gorgeous cover photo.

Cover Designer Clarice Tan with CT Cover Creations – Thank you for such a gorgeous cover design. I'm grateful for your friendship and kindness you've shown me. I have never worked with someone so professional and truly delightful. Sending you many hugs!

Editor Mitzi Carroll – Thank you tremendously! My books wouldn't be possible without your hard work, and I absolutely love reading your comments. You take my work and make it shine!

My Formatter Max Henry – Thank you for making my work look professional and beautiful, you are immensely talented, and I'm very grateful.

My PA'S Abbey Neil-Clark and Lindsay Lupher – You've both helped me so much, I can't wait to see what the future brings. Thank you for listening to my rambling and for the continued support.

Sapphire's Naughty Princesses – You ladies are brilliant, thank you for everything that you do to help promote my work and for all of your support and encouragement. Some days it's one of you that keeps me writing my next book, excited to bring you a small escape in this world. Thank you for giving me a piece of your heart, I adore you!

My blogger friends –YOU ARE AMAZING! I LOVE YOU! No really, I do!!! You take a new chance on me with each book and in return share my passion with the world. You never truly get enough credit, and I'm forever grateful!

STAY UP TO DATE WITH
Sapphire

EMAIL

authorsapphireknight@yahoo.com

WEBSITE

www.authorsapphireknight.com

FACEBOOK

www.facebook.com/AuthorSapphireKnight

CPSIA information can be obtained
at www.ICGtesting.com
Printed in the USA
LVOW08s2150091116
512359LV00013B/499/P